"MY DEAREST RUTH"

Stuffy looked around carefully, as if to make sure that no one was listening, then lowered his voice. "You know what would be really funny? What if Ruth the Doof started getting love letters from Mr. Ryan?"

I began to giggle. I could picture it. I could see Ruth's face getting all red and her pale little eyes opening so wide they nearly popped out of her head.

"It sounds like a mean trick," I said. But I giggled again. I couldn't help it. I thought of yesterday afternoon at Ruth's. I remembered her embarrassing me in front of Sheila, Teddy, and B. G. I thought of how it would feel to share the laughter with someone, instead of being the one who was snickered at. And Stuffy wanted *me* to help him.

"I'll do it!" I said.

He grabbed my hand and pumped it hard.

We were in this together, like friends. Friends to The End.

Or—I thought suddenly—partners in crime.

ANYTHING
FOR A
FRIEND

ELLEN
CONFORD

BANTAM BOOKS

TORONTO • NEW YORK • LONDON • SYDNEY • AUCKLAND

RL 5, IL age 11 and up

This low-priced Bantam Book
has been completely reset in a typeface
designed for easy reading, and was printed
from new plates. It contains the complete
text of the original hardcover edition.
NOT ONE WORD HAS BEEN OMITTED.

ANYTHING FOR A FRIEND

A Bantam Book / published by arrangement with
Little, Brown & Company

PRINTING HISTORY

Little, Brown edition published April 1979

The Starfire logo is a registered
trademark of Bantam Books, Inc. Registered in U.S. Patent and
Trademark Office and elsewhere.

Bantam edition / September 1987

Bantam Books are published by Bantam Books, Inc. Its trademark,
consisting of the words "Bantam Books" and the portrayal of a rooster, is
Registered in U.S. Patent and Trademark Office and in other countries.
Marca Registrada. Bantam Books, Inc., 666 Fifth Avenue, New York, New
York 10103.

PRINTED IN THE UNITED STATES OF AMERICA

O   0 9 8 7 6 5 4 3 2

To Michael,
for telling me about
Phil Rizzuto's roommate.

O N E

The first time I saw Stafford W. Sternwood he was doing something weird with worms.

We'd only been in Crestwood a week. I was sort of exploring the new neighborhood and finding that there wasn't all that much to explore. The houses looked a lot alike, the streets looked a lot alike, and unless you knew your way around, it was very easy to get lost.

Which I did.

I guess I began to walk around in circles, because I passed Daffodil Lane three times before I knew for sure that I wasn't going the right way.

All the streets had flower names: Daisy Court, Camellia Drive, Rhododendron Road. I thought that was pretty sickening. Our house was on Sweetpea Street, which made me want to gag, but my mother pointed out that we were lucky, because we could have bought a house in another development where they named all the streets after birds, and *that* was on Titwillow Way.

So it was no wonder that I couldn't keep all those flowers straight in my head. Do I turn left at Tulip? Right at Zinnia? No matter what I did, I kept winding up on Daffodil Lane.

Everything was so quiet. It was the last week of summer and I guess everyone was away or something, because there were hardly any kids around and no one my age.

I was beginning to get this really sick feeling in my stomach, knowing I was lost and not having any money with me to call my mother, even if I found a pay phone somewhere. I hated this place, just like I knew I would before we came here. It was dull and deserted and nobody cared about a lost kid who could go around in circles forever until she dropped dead from hunger and tiredness.

And that's when I saw Stafford W. Sternwood. He was squatting on the sidewalk with a stick in his hand, talking to something on the ground. He hadn't been there the first two times I went by, so for a minute I thought maybe I wasn't going around in circles anymore. But I looked up at the street sign and, sure enough, I was back on Daffodil Lane again.

Well, at least he can tell me how to get back to my house, I thought. I walked toward him. He was kind of plump—not really fat, but sort of bulge-y and he had blond hair that looked like it had been cut around a bowl. When I reached him I could see that he was bending over two worms and poking at them gently with a stick.

He saw my legs and looked up, squinting at me through his glasses.

"What are you doing to those poor worms?" I asked.

"What does it look like I'm doing?"

"It looks like you're poking them with a stick," I said.

"That shows how much you know. I'm training them."

"Training them to do what?"

"Wrestle." He stood up with a little groan and stamped his feet, as if they were asleep. "I don't think I'm doing it right. Every time I try to tangle them together, Killer Krause wriggles away."

I stared at him. Was he kidding?

"I never heard of worms wrestling before."

"Of course not. I invented it. I think worm wrestling could be a great new sport."

"The worms don't seem to like it much," I said. Both worms were slithering off in opposite directions. The boy reached down and plucked them off the sidewalk. He held them in his palm for me to see.

"This one is Killer Krause," he said, "and this one is Irving the Masked Marvel."

"Where's his mask?"

"I haven't made it yet. If he won't wrestle, I don't think he's going to hold still for wearing a mask."

"Then how do you tell them apart?"

"To tell you the truth, I don't. But it doesn't really matter. They don't come when they're called anyway."

He took a little box out of his pocket and opened it. He slipped Irving and Killer into the box, closed it and stuck it back into his pocket."

3

"What's your name?" he asked.

I sighed. "Wallis. With an 'i-s' Wallis Greene."

"That's a weird name for a girl."

I don't know how many people have said that to me. But this time, I didn't feel so bad about it. After all, here was a kid who named two worms Killer Krause and Irving the Masked Marvel and was trying to teach them to wrestle. Compared to that, "Wallis" sounded almost ordinary.

"My grandmother named me after a duchess," I added. I always have to explain my name because everyone thinks it's a boy's name. If we didn't have to move so much, I think I would have saved myself about a hundred explanations.

"What's yours?" I asked.

"Stafford Sternwood," he said. "Stafford W. Sternwood."

"What does the W stand for?"

"Winston."

I felt even less bad about my name.

"Do they call you Wally?" he asked.

"No!" I snapped. Wally sounds like an eight-foot-six basketball player. A couple of people started to call me Wally back in Indianapolis, but I set them straight right away.

"Well, what do your friends call you?" he asked.

I don't have any friends. We never stay in one place long enough for me to have any friends. I've lived in San Francisco, Denver, Indianapolis, Philadelphia, and now New York. When you're always the new person in school, you don't find that many friends.

But I didn't tell any of that to Stafford. "Just call me Wallis," I said.

"You new here?"

"Yeah. We just moved in last week."

"How old are you?"

"Eleven. How old are you?"

"Me too. Maybe we'll be in the same class."

I almost forgot that I was feeling rotten a couple of minutes ago. But I still didn't know how to get home.

"Oh, it's easy," Stafford said. "Just go back up this street, turn right, then go three blocks—I think it's three blocks—let's see, Rhododendron, Azalea, Larkspur—oh, maybe I better show you."

He led me back to Sweetpea Street.

"Which house is yours?"

"That one," I pointed. "The yellow one. Sixteen-thirty-two."

"Oh boy!" he said, suddenly excited. "You bought the Tucker house?"

"If that's the Tucker house we did," I said. "I don't know who we bought it from."

"Didn't they *tell* you? You really don't *know?*"

"Tell me what?"

"You really don't know!" Stafford said.

"How do I know if I know or not unless you tell me what it is I don't know!"

"Maybe they don't want you to know," he said thoughtfully. "Maybe I shouldn't tell you."

"Tell me what?"

"About the murder."

T W O

"Ma!" I yelled. "Ma, where are you?"

"Up here!" she yelled back. "Why are you yelling?"

I raced up the stairs and found her in the master bedroom, where she and my grandmother were hanging curtains. My grandmother, who lives in Brooklyn, was staying with us for a week, helping us to get settled. She was really excited that we were finally living in New York.

"Why didn't you tell me someone was murdered in this house?"

My grandmother dropped her end of the curtain. "Murdered! Lainie, who was murdered?"

My mother sighed and blew the hair out of her eyes. "How about a nice glass of iced tea?" she suggested. "It's really hot up here. The first thing your father is going to do when he gets home tonight is install that air conditioner."

"Mother!"

"Lainie, *who was murdered in this house?*"

"It wasn't a murder, exactly," my mother said. "More like a *crime passionnel.*" She pronounced it "cream passyonell," which made it sound like a French pastry.

"I don't know what that is," I said, "but did somebody kill somebody here?"

"Well . . . yes."

My grandmother dropped into a chair near the window. "You bought a house that somebody was *murdered* in? Are you crazy?"

"Why didn't you tell me?" I wailed. "Why did you buy it?"

"It was dirt cheap," my mother said weakly.

"I'll bet it was dirt cheap!" my grandmother cried. "You think they were standing in line to buy a house where they couldn't get the bloodstains out?"

"Oh, mother, don't be so gory. There aren't any bloodstains."

"It was a nice, neat strangling?" Grandma asked.

"No. A shooting."

"But a *neat* shooting?" Grandma demanded. "Or did they clean up afterwards?"

"Mother, please. You're getting yourself all excited."

"Ma," I said, "I don't want to live in a house that somebody got shot in. It's horrible. How could you do this to me?"

I stormed out of the room and started for my own room at the end of the hall. It wasn't bad enough that I was going to be "the new kid" again, but now I was going to be the new kid who lived in the place where the murder happened. It wasn't bad enough to have to explain about being Wallis-with-an-*i-s*. Everybody would probably think the house was haunted or something and no one would ever come over, even if I did make some friends.

And what if it really was haunted? How in the world was I ever going to sleep in this place? I stopped at the door of my room. Maybe it actually happened in *my room.* I raced back down the hall.

". . . so Mrs. Tucker shot him," my mother was explaining. "There in bed."

"Where?" I demanded. "Where did Mrs. Tucker shoot him?"

"Right between the eyes," Grandma said grimly.

"Mother, please! You'll scare her."

"Oh, now, you're worried about scaring her?" Grandma said sarcastically. "When you bought the house you didn't worry?"

"*Where was he shot?*" I screamed. "*What room?*"

"This one," my mother said.

I jumped.

"You're both being very silly," she went on. "People die all the time and other people buy their houses. Now, I'm very hot and tired and I'm going downstairs to have some iced tea. In case you want to know, this is exactly why Jerry and I decided not to tell either of you about . . . it."

My grandmother looked at me and I looked at her. Then we both stared at my mother.

"Very childish," my mother continued. "Superstitious nonsense."

She backed out of the room.

Grandma frowned and didn't say anything.

Then we both looked around the large, sunny bedroom and we both jumped up at the same moment.

"Let's get out of here," she muttered. I nodded and scooted out the door with Grandma right behind me. She shut the door carefully, like something might *escape* if she didn't.

"At least *you* don't have to sleep in there," she said.

"Grandma, I don't think I'm going to sleep anywhere here at all."

My mother poured out three glasses of iced tea and set them on the kitchen table.

"I should have told you," she admitted. She put her hand on my shoulder. "It was ridiculous to think you wouldn't find out. How *did* you find out?"

"This kid told me," I said. I ignored her pleased smile. I knew she was thinking I had made a friend already. "And it was ridiculous to buy this house in the first place. That's what's ridiculous."

Grandma leaned against the kitchen counter looking thoughtful.

"I think I'll go back to Brooklyn today."

"Oh, Mother, come on. You've been in this house four days already and it didn't bother you one bit until ten minutes ago."

"Look, Lainie, it's none of my business, and I've said what I have to say about the whole thing and I'm not going to say another word about it. From my son I would expect something like this, but I thought you had more sense."

"And I thought you of all people would think it was *interesting*," my mother said. "You're such a *romantic*."

That's true. My grandmother is five foot nine and doesn't look the type, but she really is a very romantic person. It was her idea to name me after the Duchess of Windsor, for whom the King of England gave up his throne. (Before she was a duchess.) And she named my father's sister Margaret Rose, after a princess. And she's never gotten over her crush on Clark Gable, even though he's been dead for years.

She says the high point of her life was when she took a trip to California in 1949 and saw him in the Farmers' Market picking out avocados. While my grandfather—who was still alive then—grumbled, she went right up to Clark Gable and asked for his autograph and would he write "To Mae" on it?

"I thought I would faint on the spot," she says, every time she tells the story. "You know what he wrote? He wrote, 'To Mae, *affectionately*, Clark Gable.'"

She took that autograph out so many times to show people that it began to get all wrinkled, so she finally had it laminated and now she carries around the shiny, plastic autograph like it was a credit card.

"I don't think there's anything romantic about a house someone was murdered in," Grandma said. "And maybe if an acquaintance of mine who I wasn't too crazy about moved into it, I'd think it was interesting. My grandchild living at the scene of a grisly death is not interesting. But I'm not going to say another word about it."

"Doesn't anybody care what I think?" I shouted and burst into tears. I didn't know I was going to cry until I started, so I was as surprised as anyone when I began sobbing so hard that I put my head down on my arms to hide my face.

"Wallis! Oh, honey."

"Wallis, I didn't mean to upset you. I'll stay a few more days if you want."

Two arms went around my shoulders and a hand stroked my hair.

"I didn't want to move here," I sobbed. "I never wanted to move anywhere. I can never make any friends and nobody ever likes me and I'm always the new kid and I never know what they're up to in schoolwork. And now they're going to call me Weird Wallis and say I live in a haunted house."

"Oh no they won't," my mother said.

I looked up at her and swiped away some of the tears. "Oh yes they will," I cried. "You don't know kids like I do."

I started to hiccup.

"Drink some of your tea," Grandma suggested. "And hold your breath."

I just kept hiccuping. I didn't care if I hiccuped to death.

My mother wiped my hot, wet face with a paper towel.

"I know it's been hard on you, honey. But Daddy has to go where the opportunities are. It isn't easy to work yourself up the way he's been doing. He has to take the promotions that come along, or he won't get where he wants. It's no fun for me either, Wallis, to be uprooting us over and over again, even though I try to be cheerful about it."

"Well, why doesn't he think of how we feel once in a while? Why can't he just stay in the same job in the same place and not be so selfish?"

"Oh, honey, we've told you why. It's because the company likes him so much that he keeps being promoted so fast. And that's why we have to move so often. Daddy is ambitious, and he wants the best for all of us."

"If he wanted the best for you and me, he'd let us stay some place forever and not move anymore. He only cares about what's best for *him*."

My mother and Grandma gave each other one of those looks. But I didn't care what they were thinking.

"If he has a job that's satisfying to him, where he can really use his talent and ability, that will be good for all of us," my mother said.

I just shook my head. I didn't understand it, and nothing she said was going to make any difference. If my father was happy, that would be good for all of us. Why didn't it work the other way around? What if *I* was happy? How come *that* wouldn't be good for all of us? My father wanted a lot of money and an important job, but all I wanted was to live in one house that really felt like my own house and have friends that I knew would be my friends next year, and go to a school that I knew my way around in. We don't *need* a lot of money. At least, I don't. But I guess my father doesn't see it that way, and that's what I will never understand.

"Wallis." My grandmother sat down across from me. "No matter what I said about this house, don't you know how happy it makes me to have you living here? Not in this exact house, maybe—" she glanced at my mother "—but near enough to see you without having to get on a plane and travel all over the country. That means so much to me, Wallis. And even if you feel bad about everything else here, I wish you would feel just a little happy about being near me."

I jumped out of my chair and threw my arms around her.

"Oh, I do, Grandma! I didn't mean to hurt your feelings! You're the only good thing about moving to this place!"

Grandma held my hands tightly in hers, so tightly my fingers squashed together. "Maybe not," she said. "Maybe there will be other good things too. You never can tell."

I sighed and she let go of my hands. I rubbed them. Grandma is *strong.* "I can tell, Grandma." I turned away. Weird Wallis. The school joke. *Ooh, you better not go near Wallis. You know where she lives?* I've been in enough different schools to know that all the kids need is one weapon like that to make your life miserable.

"What your mother said is true, Wallis. Some people, myself not included particularly, might think it's interesting to live in a house where—well, to live in *this* house."

I looked up and found my mother staring at Grandma, as surprised as I was.

"A lot depends on your own attitude."

"Grandma is absolutely right," my mother said enthusiastically. "If *you* think it's exciting to live in a house where a famous crime occurred, the other kids will think so too. But if you give them the idea that you're ashamed of it, that's when they'll start teasing you, because they'll know you're sensitive about it. You have to act proud that you live in this house."

"I wouldn't go that far," Grandma muttered.

"Well, you know what I mean. Maybe *proud* isn't the right word."

I knew they were trying to help. I could see that they did care about how I felt. And at least my mother was admitting that I had a real problem, and that kids *do* tease other kids for the least little reason, instead of saying for the hundredth time, "Dear, you have to *be* a friend to make a friend."

But I didn't think their advice was going to do me much good.

And nothing either of them would say was going to make me sleep with the lights off tonight.

T H R E E

My father came home late, looking tired. He had to commute to the city by train and it was an hour each way. I never remember him looking so tired all the time in any of the other places we lived in.

But his face brightened up when he saw me. He always had a big smile for me, even when I didn't have one for him, and today was one of the days that I didn't.

"How's my girl?" he asked, giving me a big hug.

"Hello, Father."

He stepped back. "Uh oh. What did I do this time? Before you answer that, here." He handed me a brown paper bag. "I bought this for you."

I didn't even open the bag. "Is this a bribe?" I asked. "So I won't be mad at you?"

"When I bought it, I didn't know you *were* mad at me," he pointed out. "Go on, open it."

Inside the bag was a light blue T-shirt with a picture of a big apple on it. Skyscrapers were rising out of the apple and underneath the picture was printed "I LOVE NEW YORK."

"It's very nice," I said dully. "Thanks."

"You don't like it."

"I like it. It's very cute. I just don't agree with the message on it."

"Well, they didn't have any 'I Hate New York' shirts there, but maybe they'll make one up to order." He was trying to make a joke of it, but it wasn't funny to me. He couldn't force me to like New York, just because he bought me a shirt that said I did. I'd never wear the shirt anyway. It would be *hypocritical*.

"Try it on. Let's see if I got the right size."

"It looks like the right size," I said. "I don't have to try it on." I dropped it carelessly on the couch.

My mother and Grandma, who'd been watching and listening without saying anything, both began to talk at once.

"You must be starved," my mother said, while Grandma asked why he was so late.

We had already eaten, but my mother had a plate keeping warm for my father. The three of them went into the kitchen. I stayed in the living room with the television on, not watching the seven o'clock news.

I didn't even try to hear what they were talking about. I knew my mother would be telling my father how I found out that Mrs. Tucker shot her husband in their bedroom. And he would figure that was the reason I was mad at him.

Well, if he wanted to kid himself that that was the only reason, I didn't care. That was just the *latest* reason and my mother and Grandma—and even he—knew perfectly well all the other reasons.

He knew, but he didn't understand. Or he didn't want to understand. Either way, he wasn't going to change. Maybe it was easier for him not to understand, because then he wouldn't feel like he had to do anything to make things better.

But how could he know how I felt? Grandma told me the whole story of his life, practically from the time of his birth. He was born in Brooklyn, grew up in Brooklyn, went to elementary school in Brooklyn, went to high school at Brooklyn Tech and even went to Brooklyn College.

How could someone like that ever really feel what it is to be shifted from school to school so many times that you never know from one year to the next what *state* you'll be living in, let alone how to walk to your school? Maybe he really believed, like he was always telling me, that it was fun and exciting and adventurous to see so many new places, and that it was a terrific opportunity, if only I would take advantage of it.

Maybe it *was* fun—for him. And if I had spent twenty-one years in the same place, maybe I'd think it was exciting to see new things. But at the rate we moved around, I never got to spend more than a year and a half in one place and I couldn't even imagine how it would feel to grow up knowing that where you were today you would be next year, and the kids you knew now, you would go all through school with.

My father still has some friends from his childhood that he sees once in a while. Maybe he's also better at making friends than I am, but I haven't got one friend, from all the places we lived in, who still writes to me. In fact, only two people ever did write to me after we moved; one was from Denver and one from Indianapolis, but they stopped writing after the first couple of times. We were never that good friends anyway, and I was very young then.

And my father never had to stand up in front of the whole class and have the teacher say, "This is Wallis. She's new to our class and I know we're all going to like her very much." I could never look back at those twenty or thirty pairs of staring eyes for more than a second or two. I always ended up by ducking my head down and trying to keep from showing how self-conscious I felt. I've examined more classroom floors than most people ever notice in their whole lives. All the while I would know, and know that the other kids knew, that they *weren't* going to like me very much. It was just like my father giving me an "I LOVE NEW YORK" T-shirt. That wasn't going to make me love New York and the teacher's saying "We're all going to like her" was definitely not going to make the class like *me*.

Then there was my name. "Wallis," most of the teachers said, "what an unusual name for a girl." In the second grade I said, "My grandmother named me after a duchess," trying to explain my name when the teacher introduced me. The whole class snickered. They didn't even know what a duchess was. One boy thought it was a kind of cheese.

After that I never said anything about my name when I stood up there in front of the whole class. I just waited until I could slip into my seat and scrunch down, hoping they'd stop looking at me. I explained later, if anyone asked me. I even had to explain why my grandmother had named me, instead of my mother and father. Since I've never really understood that myself, it was kind of hard to explain it to the other kids.

It's not like my grandmother has piles of money that she'll leave us in her will if we do everything she wants. She just has a very strong and very romantic personality. And my mother always insisted that she liked the name Wallis too, and that Grandma could never have talked her into it if Mom didn't agree that Wallis was a lovely name.

The tears were beginning to well up in my eyes again. I kept trying to tell myself that since I was starting school at the beginning of the year, at least I wouldn't have to stand up there and be introduced. That was a definite plus. But living in the Tucker house was going to be a definite minus. *Weird Wallis.*

They were up to the stock market report on the news. Right through the Dow-Jones averages I could almost hear the taunting voices of my new classmates.

"Weird Wallis. Hey, see any ghosts last night? I'll bet she sleeps with a night-light."

Why couldn't I be Mary Smith and grow up in Springfield, Illinois, and never be noticed by anyone for anything except perhaps for being extremely pretty? (Which I'm not. I've also never lived in Springfield, Illinois, but it sounds nice and ordinary and the kind of place you live in all your life.)

We would have a sweet, white house where my best friend and I would make cookies and climb up into the tree house my father would build in the crook of the big old elm tree in the backyard. And we'd exchange secrets and maybe even take a Blood Oath to be friends forever, although that probably wouldn't be necessary, since we would *know* we'd be friends forever.

And every day she would call for me and we would walk to school together. Or, if we went on class trips, she would be my partner on the bus.

That doesn't seem like so much to want. Some people want *things*—mopeds, skateboards, stereos, guitars—things you need a lot of money for. I wasn't asking for anything like that. I don't even care about *things*. If I did, maybe my father would be able to understand me better. He cares about *things*. He knows "the value of money." He would probably understand me wanting something big and expensive. What I want most of all in the world doesn't cost anything—and I guess that's why he doesn't understand me.

By the time the news was over I was feeling so rotten that I didn't even bother to get up and change the channel to something more interesting than "Untamed Wilderness: A Trip Down the Amazon." What difference did it make?

My parents and Grandma came into the living room and sat down. I could feel them all looking at me, though my eyes were fixed on the program I wasn't watching. It was like they were all waiting to say something, but nobody wanted to go first.

Finally my father began. "Wallis . . ."

"Yes, Father?" I didn't look up. If he really loved me, we'd be in that little white house in Springfield, Illinois, right now. If he really cared about how I felt—

"Oh, honey, don't call me 'Father' like that."

"I'm sorry. *Sir*," I added, in a whisper.

"Your mother told me you heard about the—the—*incident* in the bedroom."

"Hah!" snorted Grandma. "You make it sound like someone tripped on a scatter rug. But I've said all I'm going to say on the subject. I won't say another word."

"Good!" my father snapped. "Now, honey, listen. The real estate agent who showed me the house never said a word about the—the—"

"Murder," I said. "I know the word. I watch the news."

"All right, the murder. Although, actually, I think it was manslaughter. I mean, at the trial."

"That makes all the difference," said Grandma.

"*In any case*," my father went on loudly, "she showed me the house and she said she knew it was just what we were looking for and it *was*. I knew you and your mother would love it. It had everything we needed, it's in a nice neighborhood, all the appliances were included—"

"Mrs. Tucker having no use for her refrigerator in Sing Sing," Grandma muttered.

"It has a beautiful, big room for you," my father went on.

"And it was dirt cheap," I added.

"Money was a secondary consideration," he said firmly.

That'll be the day. I looked over at my mother, who had said only a few hours ago that the main reason they bought the house was because it was cheap.

"Well, the price was a consideration, of course," she said, like she knew what I was thinking. "But not the *main* consideration."

"Anyhow, I liked it so much that I called your

mother in Philadelphia right from the agent's office and told her all about it and she said, it sounds perfect, I should grab it. So I put a deposit down on it and signed a paper that said I intended to buy it and that's when the agent told me about the—about Mr. Tucker."

I sat up in the chair, startled. "You mean, she didn't tell you until *after* you signed the paper?"

"That's right."

"That wasn't fair!"

"No, it probably wasn't, but it was legal. Anyway, I liked the house so much, that even when she told me, I wasn't that upset. People die all the time, you know. Houses don't stay empty just because someone has died in them."

"Not if they die from old age, no," my grandmother agreed.

"Couldn't you un-sign?" I asked. "Did you absolutely have to buy the house?"

My parents looked at each other for what seemed like a long time before they answered.

Finally my father said, "I think I could have gotten out of it. But, honey, I didn't want to at that point. Remember, I had been up here four times looking for a good house and the only thing that I saw that was remotely possible was that little dinky one on Titwillow. Time was running out. And this one was so right for us. I knew you'd love it—and you did, up till today."

"I never loved it," I said.

"Well, you liked it."

"I didn't even like it. I just said it was okay."

"Wallis," my mother said, "for you that's as good as liking it." She smiled.

"And I'm sure no one's going to make fun of you because you live here," my father finished.

I slumped back down in the chair. I could feel another pep talk coming on. More of "You have to be a friend to make a friend," and "You shouldn't be so *prickly*, Wallis. It puts people off." And "Dear, you're much too sensitive. You take things too personally."

At least I knew my father hadn't deliberately decided on this house, knowing that there was a bloody history attached to it. Maybe he should have tried to get out of it after he knew, but, being my father, he probably didn't realize how I would feel about it. After all, he didn't understand me in most ways, so why should he even think twice about this?

"Yeah. Well," I said at last, "I guess it's not *entirely* your fault. The agent did pull a fast one on you."

"They ought to take away her license," Grandma nodded. "A sharpie like that. And you remember what I told you, Wallis, about your own attitude. How you see yourself is how others will see you."

"I'll remember, Grandma." I sighed. I was sure I was in for a long evening of good advice, but instead my father turned the channel to a police show and we all sat and watched car chases and didn't say anything for a while.

"Time for bed, honey," my mother said. "'Way past time, really."

I looked over to the staircase and imagined the dark, gloomy hall upstairs.

"I'm not sleepy." I yawned.

"Oh, yes you are. Do you want me to go up with you?"

"I'm exhausted," said Grandma. "I think I'll go to bed myself. Let's go, Wallis." She hauled me off my chair with one strong hand gripping me on the arm, and led the way upstairs.

"First of all," she said when we got to the top of the stairs, "we'll leave the hall light on. And you leave your door open and I'll leave my door open. I might even sleep with my light on."

"Oh, Grandma, you're not really scared too, are you?" I nearly laughed, even though I kept looking around as if something was lurking in the shadows.

"No, dear, of course I'm not scared. There's nothing to be afraid of. Do you want to use the bathroom first?"

"Grandma," I whispered, "did they tell you how *it* happened?"

She pulled me into her room, quickly flipping on the light switch. "It really *is* interesting," she said, sounding almost excited. "You see, Mrs. Tucker was out at her regular Tuesday night bowling league. She bowled with a team from her office called the Compton Business Machinettes."

"Machine-ettes?"

"Right. Anyway, there she was, just about to try for a seven-ten split, when she overhears a woman talking in the lane next to hers. And this woman is talking about Mr. Tucker, her husband."

"How does she know that?"

"Because of all the things the woman said. It could only be Mr. Tucker. Anyway, this woman is saying that Mr. Tucker has been seeing another woman and everyone in the whole office knows about it except Mrs. Tucker."

"Did he work for Compton Business Machines too?"

"No, I think he worked in an accounting firm. Anyway, so she said she felt really sorry for Mrs.

Tucker, because Mr. Tucker was making a fool of her in front of the whole world. So Mrs. Tucker went home and took a gun from the top of the back of the linen closet, where Mr. Tucker kept it in case of emergencies, and sneaked up the stairs and shot him in the head while he was sound asleep."

"Boy, she really must have been angry."

"Yes, dear, I think she was probably pretty angry."

"I would have woken him up first," I said thoughtfully. "I mean, I'd want him to know *why* I was shooting him."

"I agree," said Grandma. "I don't see any point in murdering someone who you're trying to teach a lesson to without telling him why first."

I looked around her room. "You don't suppose . . ."

"No, Wallis, I really don't think so. Anyway, it's your parents' room he'd be in if his spirit is still hanging around, which it certainly isn't. And they're not a bit afraid, and they've been in there a week with no problems."

"I never believed in ghosts," I said. "But I never lived in any place where there might be one before."

"Don't worry. I'll be right here and we'll leave the lights on."

Wallis sleeps with a night-light.

"Grandma?" I was in no hurry to be alone in my room. "Did she make the seven-ten split?"

"You mother didn't say, dear. But in Mrs. Tucker's condition, I would have rolled a gutter ball."

I got into bed a few minutes later. The hall light was on but I had closed my door. I hate to sleep with lights on nearby. Most of the time, ever since I've been a little kid, I'm never afraid of the dark, and I like it to be *really* dark when I go to sleep. Really dark is better than shadowy, anyway, because really dark is too dark to imagine that you see strange shapes in the corners of the room and near the closet.

The light from the hall filtered in, a thin little line under my door. There was a moon out, but not a very bright one. My window blinds made lines on the wall next to my bed. I could see enough to notice that my closet door was open a couple of inches. I hesitated only a moment, then leaped out of bed, pushed it shut and dove back into bed.

I pulled the sheet up to my chin. It was still pretty hot up here so I had no blanket. My parents walked up the stairs, they were getting ready to go to bed too. The stairs creaked.

My mother talked in a low voice to Grandma. Then there were bathroom sounds, then their door closed and there were bed-squeaking sounds. The hall light was still on. But now there were no sounds at all.

My head darted back and forth on the pillow, looking from one side of my shadowy room to the other. I must have looked like a radar scope in one of those science fiction movies—a big bowl, always scanning the skies for UFO's. Back and forth, back and forth.

The stairs creaked again. But this time there was no one on them.

I sat up in bed. I was not going to get to sleep tonight. Maybe I would sleep tomorrow night, maybe not till the night after that, but tonight I was definitely not going to get to sleep. If I opened my door, the light from the hall would shine in, but I hated going to bed with my door open.

_____

I snapped on the lamp next to my bed and reached for my transistor radio. I turned it on low and clutched it right next to my ear. I leaned back on my pillow and stared at the blue checked curtains my mother had put up yesterday. My eyes grew heavier and heavier, but I would never get to sleep with a lamp on, even if I wasn't scared of the ghost of Mr. Tucker coming back to the scene of his death.

A talk-show host was discussing communication with Those on the Other Side. I held the radio even closer to my ear. I hoped Mr. Tucker wasn't listening. I didn't want him to pick up any pointers.

Even with the lamp on, there were dark corners in my room. Hot as it was, I pulled the sheet over my head and scrunched down under it with my radio.

Wallis sleeps with a night-light. Wallis sleeps with a night-light.

F O U R

My mother and Grandma had all sorts of advice for me on the first day of school. It started with "But you have to eat *something*, Wallis. You can't go to school on an empty stomach."

"If I eat anything, Grandma, I'll throw up. Please don't force me."

Then they went on to how I should smile and be friendly. I shouldn't be standoffish. I shouldn't be touchy about my name. I should make everyone think that living in a house where a murder took place was just about the greatest thing since peanut butter.

It was a good thing my father had already gone to work. If I had three people giving me helpful hints, I would have blown all my fuses, like a computer destroying itself. "OVERLOAD! OVERLOAD! I CANNOT COMPUTE."

I nearly blew up anyhow, and it was almost a relief to get out of the house, even though it meant I was now on my way to Briar Lane Elementary School—if I didn't get lost. My mother had registered me there a couple of days ago, when my records came in from my last school, and the principal, Mrs. Costa, had shown me the room I was assigned to and told me the name of my teacher, Mr. Ryan.

The school wasn't huge, but it was two stories high and sort of sprawled around and I wasn't at all sure that I could ever find room 203 again, even if I found the school. My mother wanted to drive me but I said no, I would manage, even though I had no idea whether I would manage or not.

I walked up Sweetpea Street slowly, as slowly as I could. *The condemned prisoner walks the last mile to the Electric Chair.*

At the corner I saw a bunch of younger kids, maybe second and third graders. I figured if I followed them I ought to be all right. They turned the corner and I hurried a bit so I wouldn't lose them. I didn't want to walk with them of course, not with little kids, but I had to keep them in sight to find my way to school.

Just then I saw Stafford W. Sternwood turning down Sweetpea Street walking toward me. Why was he walking this way? I looked around, confused. Was I walking in the wrong direction? Were the little kids walking in the wrong direction? Did they go to a different school, maybe a parochial school or something? No, I was at least sure that I had to walk up Sweetpea Street and turn right; that much I remembered.

"Hi, Wallis."

"Hi. What are you doing here?"

"I thought you might want help getting to school. Being new and all. You were lost last week, so—"

"I can find my way," I said. He must think I'm a moron or something. Then, I could almost hear my mother's voice, "Don't be so *prickly*, Wallis."

"Well. Thanks."

"You're welcome. Just follow me."

I followed him. I didn't say anything for a while and neither did he. But I began thinking. This is my first day of school and *I'm walking to school with someone*. That had never happened before in my whole life. I should be *grateful*. And Stafford could even help me find my room.

"What teacher do you have?" he asked.

"Mr. Ryan."

"Hey, we're in the same class!"

This was really incredible. Another First. I would actually know someone in my class before I got there. I felt my stomach settle down a little. It didn't exactly stop fluttering and jumping, but at least I didn't feel like I would be sick if the smallest morsel of food passed my lips.

"Mr. Ryan is supposed to be really funny," Stafford said. "But this kid I know told me that he doesn't stand for any fooling around."

I wasn't sure I liked the sound of Mr. Ryan. Really funny teachers might make fun of you and the kind that don't stand for any fooling around are usually mean. The combination of both kinds of teacher in one person sounded a little scary. Also, I never had a man teacher before. There were going to be a whole lot of Firsts for me today. I had a feeling I wouldn't like most of the rest of them.

"How are the worms coming?" I asked finally.

"Oh, not so good. I'm still working on them, though. I brought them with me." He patted his pants pocket. "Figured I'd have some time after lunch. You have to keep up the training every day, you know. A couple of times a day, in fact. They have very short attention spans."

Was he kidding? Was this a big joke that Stafford was putting over on me, or did he really think he was inventing a whole new sport? I still couldn't tell.

"Anyway," he went on, "they sure won't be ready for Madison Square Garden for a while."

I could see the school now, halfway up the long block we were turning on to. Hundreds of kids were surging toward it. I thought if you took aerial films of it from the Goodyear blimp, it would look like one of those cartoons where people from all directions are streaming into Yankee Stadium for the Big Game.

I swallowed a couple of times. Then, quickly, before Stafford could see how nervous I was, I asked, "Isn't Madison Square Garden awfully big?"

It didn't really matter whether or not he was putting me on. The important thing was, I wasn't alone.

"How are the people going to be able to see the worms?"

"I have that all figured out," Stafford said confidently. "I'm going to give out special glasses, like they did for Three-D movies in the fifties. Cardboard, you know, that you just throw away afterwards. But these'll be *magnifying* glasses, so you'll be able to see the worms enlarged, maybe a hundred times bigger than life."

At any other time I would have said that was the stupidest idea I ever heard, but now we were heading for the steps at the far wing of the school. The pale yellow brick building seemed squat and ugly, and the double doors, green metal and wide open, formed a giant mouth that was waiting to swallow me up.

Metal letters over the door spelled "BRIAR ANE SCHOOL."

"The 'L' is missing," I told Stafford. I was jostled from behind by a couple of kids who ran around us and up the steps as if they were being chased.

"Someone's always stealing the L," Stafford said. "I think they do it just so they can say they got the L out of Briar Lane. Get it?"

I shook my head.

"Get the L out? You get it?"

"Oh. Oh, yeah." I tried to chuckle, like I appreciated the joke. But I wasn't feeling very chuckle-y.

"Hey, Stuffy!" A boy pushed in between us and gave Stafford a jab with his elbow that nearly knocked him into the stair railing.

"Hey, Packy."

"You got Ryan too, right?"

"Yeah."

We got to the top of the stairs and started down a long hall. I kept track of how to get to room 203. I knew that after today, when everyone met up with their old friends again, I wouldn't have anybody walking with me. I'd better know how to find my room myself.

The kid named Packy and Stafford, who, I guessed, everyone called Stuffy, were talking a mile a minute, so I just sort of followed a little bit behind them, looking at room numbers, watching the kids darting down the hall and taking note of all the thin spots in the pale green paint on the walls.

"Here we are," Stafford said suddenly. I stopped, before I bumped into them. The other boy looked at me curiously, like he hadn't realized that I was with Stafford.

"This is Wallis Greene," said Stafford. "She's new. She's in our class too."

"Hi," said Packy carelessly. He had a thin, pointy face and very dark, straight hair. He hardly glanced at me. I waited, but he didn't say a thing about my name.

The room was half full of kids and a man with light brown hair and a blue suit was perched on the big desk in front. I looked around for a seat. The desks were lined up in pairs and almost everybody seemed to be talking to someone.

Right in the middle of the room about six girls were clustered together. They stopped their jabbering to turn and stare at me as I walked slowly down the row to an empty desk. One girl was sitting alone in the next aisle and she smiled at me eagerly, almost like she was hoping I'd sit down next to her.

She had short, frizzy brown hair and pale, almost colorless little eyes. And she was fat. She seemed to be the only one in the class who had a looseleaf notebook, two pencils, and a pen neatly arranged on her desk, as if she couldn't wait for the teacher to begin piling on the work.

I didn't know her, yet I recognized her right away. I had seen her in Denver and in Indianapolis and in Philadelphia, and I figured there had to be one in every class in every school all over the country.

She was The Girl Nobody Liked.

If you wanted to make fun of someone, you picked on her. If you wanted to play a mean trick on someone, you played it on her. If you had a party and invited every girl in the class but one, she was the one you left out. In jump rope, she either had to turn the rope the whole time, or not play at all. And if she did get to jump, it was only after everyone else had had their turn, and she always missed within ten seconds. She got chosen last for everything else, too, and then the team that got her grumbled about having to be stuck with her.

I felt sorry for her. I always did. But after getting too friendly with The Girl Nobody Liked in Indianapolis, and being The Other Girl Nobody Liked for half a year, I knew I had to be careful. I had been to anxious to make friends with someone—anyone—that year. That's how I had gotten stuck with Brenda, and once I was stuck with her, none of the other girls would be friends with me.

I felt sorry for Brenda, just like I knew I was going to feel sorry for this girl too, whoever she was, but I'd feel a lot worse if I ended up as one of this class's Brendas.

So I just smiled a little at her and sat down next to an empty desk, pretending that I didn't understand the eager, welcoming look on her face.

One of the girls behind me tapped me on the shoulder. I turned around, startled.

"You're new, aren't you?" she asked. She had long, blond hair and pink-tinted glasses. The other girls were looking from her to me and I realized that this girl was *important*. There's one of those in every class too.

Even if I was starting on the first day of school,

along with everyone else, I was still the new girl. These kids must have known each other since kindergarten to spot me right away like that.

"Don't be so prickly, Wallis. Be friendly." I tried to smile. "Yeah. We just moved in."

She wore a dusky blue shirt and a flowered skirt. I was glad, at least, that I was dressed right. Except for the colors, my clothes were practically the same as hers.

"I'm Sheila Denton," she said coolly. "This is Teddy Zeller and B. G. Blaine." She pointed to two girls, one next to her and one in the next row. Teddy smiled, like she really meant it. She had short, straight light brown hair, dark, dark eyes and a terrific tan. B. G. was tall, even sitting down, and very thin. She had red-blond hair and a sprinkling of freckles over the bridge of her nose and under her eyes. I knew they were the next most important ones. Then Sheila introduced the other girls sitting around and watching us, but I figured I'd better keep track of Sheila, Teddy, and B. G., no matter who else I forgot.

"And don't ask me what B. G. stands for," the tall girl warned. "It's just *awful*."

"She's dying for you to ask her," Teddy said, her eyes sparkling. "She always says it's awful, but she always tells you."

"Well, it can't be as bad as mine," I said, warmed by Teddy's smiled. These three were actually talking to me. They were being *friendly*. My stomach almost stopped fluttering. Maybe it was going to be different here. Thank goodness I'd been smart enough not to sit down next to the fat girl!

A loud bell rang. The PA system squawked, and the principal, Mrs. Costa, led us in the Pledge of Alle-

---

giance. Then she wished a happy first day of school to all and hoped that our year would be educational and productive.

Mr. Ryan called the roll.

Packy turned out to be George Packwood. B. G. was Bianca, but I still didn't know what the "G" stood for.

"Wallis Greene." I raised my hand, like he'd told us to, and said, "Here."

He looked surprised. "Oh. I thought you were a boy."

I put my hand down. Everyone snickered and I could feel my face turning hot.

"No, I see, Wallis with an *I*." I wished he would stop and just go on to the next person. "Like Wallis Simpson, right?"

I nodded, not looking up from my desk top. Why did he have to keep on about it like this? No one knew who Wallis Simpson was, and everyone was staring at me. Even without looking up, I could feel their eyes on me.

Finally he went on with the roll. A moment later, a folded piece of paper was stuck over my shoulder and fluttered into my lap.

I turned around. Sheila was nodding. I opened the note.

"Who is Wallice Simpson?" it read.

My heart thumping, I reached into my skirt pocket for a pen to answer the note. I couldn't believe that Sheila was taking so much interest in me. I wanted to answer the note *just right*, so I thought for a moment before I wrote:

"Would you believe, a duchess?" I was going to write, "Wallis with an *i-s*," but I didn't want to correct her. She'd find out eventually how it was spelled. Then, hoping to get another note from her, I added, "What does the G in B. G. stand for?" I dropped the paper back over my shoulder.

A minute later it landed in my lap again. "Ask B. G.," it read. "It's her name."

Cold, just like Sheila's voice. All the good feelings drained out of me in a second. I had been too pushy. I was nosy. It was okay for them to be nosy, because they weren't new. They were entitled to ask all the questions they wanted. My job was just to answer them.

Mr. Ryan finished calling the roll. "These seating arrangements are temporary," he announced. "In a couple of days I'll assign permanent seats. We're going to alternate rows of boys and girls."

The whole class groaned out loud protests.

"You don't like the idea?" Mr. Ryan asked, his face innocent.

"NO!" everyone yelled.

"Good. Then I know I'm doing the right thing."

Sarcastic. The very worst kind of teacher to have. Only a few minutes before I had been warming myself with Teddy's smile, and now I was cold and alone again. Sheila wasn't going to send me any more notes and if I thought she was going to be my friend I was just kidding myself. And I would cringe every time Mr. Ryan called on me, because I would never know what he would say to make the class laugh at me if I gave the wrong answer. Even if the rest of the class hates the teacher too, they'll always laugh when he makes a joke at your expense. For one thing, they're always relieved it's you and not them he's picking on.

The morning dragged on. Mr. Ryan handed out books and told us to have them covered by tomorrow. I took out my little spiral notebook from my skirt pocket and copied down the stuff he told us we had to get. No one whispered to me or passed me any more notes.

There was still no one sitting at the desk next to me. Stuffy was over near the windows next to Packy. Even the fat girl, whose name was Ruth Cutler, didn't turn around again to look at me. I was completely alone in a class full of people.

They hadn't even found out about the Tucker house yet.

At eleven-thirty I followed the rest of the class to the lunchroom.

Some kids brought lunch from home and some lined up at the hot lunch counter. I had a dollar with me so I went to the counter. I got a pizza and a salad and some juice and milk and an apple. Then I looked around for a place to sit.

The room was huge, but already crowded with people, and so noisy that you could probably set off ten sticks of dynamite right in the center of it and no one would notice. There were rows and rows of tables and benches, most of them already filled with kids.

I saw Sheila, Teddy, and B. G. at one table. There were two empty spots opposite them. I just stood there with my tray, looking at those two vacant seats. I could ask to sit with them, but Sheila might tell me they were saving the seats. And I didn't want to force myself on them. After my note, Sheila already thought I was too pushy.

Suddenly I wanted to drop my tray and run out of

the lunchroom and down the stairs and out of Briar Ane School and not stop until I got home. Only, I didn't have a home. I lived in the Tucker house, and it was just a house that once belonged to the Tuckers and would eventually belong to someone else after we moved again.

But there was no point in running away from the school. In the first place, I'd just have to come back again tomorrow, and in the second place, we'd be moving again so that all I had to do to get away from Briar Ane School was to *wait*.

Okay, I was lonely and scared and didn't know where to carry my tray. But it wasn't that different from any other time I'd been the new girl. I was used to the way I felt. Even though it never got any easier, even if I always felt this awful, cold lump in the pit of my stomach for at least the first day—and sometimes longer—it was no surprise anymore. I just had to live through it one more time. And after this time, there'd be the next time, and after that—but I wasn't going to think about that now. I couldn't stand in the middle of the lunchroom holding that tray any longer. I must look like an idiot.

Sheila glanced up and saw me and said something to B. G. She looked up too and I waited, hoping for just a second that they would wave to me.

Of course they didn't. They went back to their own lunches, talking and laughing between bites. I felt tears come to my eyes, and squeezed them back, hard. I'd been right not to try and sit with them. I spotted one empty space at a table across the room and I hurried toward it. It didn't matter where I sat, as long as I didn't stand there looking dumb and friendless any longer.

I slid into the seat at the end of the table and found myself right next to Ruth.

"Hi!" she said happily. "'Did you see me waving?"

Oh, no. I looked around to see if Sheila or Teddy or B. G. saw where I was sitting, but they were farther toward the front of the room, with their backs to our table.

"No. I didn't notice." I bit into my pizza. It was cold by now but I didn't mind. I was hungry and there was nothing in my stomach but that cold rock, which made me feel hungrier.

"You're new here, aren't you?" Ruth asked.

Brilliant deduction. I would almost rather be sitting at a table all by myself than next to Ruth. I knew I wasn't going to like her any more than anyone else in the class did, even if she was trying to be nice. *Especially* if she was trying to be nice.

"We just moved in. During the summer." I stuffed my mouth full of pizza. Couldn't she see I was trying to eat?

"Where do you live?"

"On Sweetpea Street," I said, after I swallowed everything. *"You have to be a friend to make a friend."* My mother's voice echoed in my head. But I don't *want* this friend. I can't afford this friend. If Ruth latched onto me, I wouldn't have any other friends as long as I stayed in this school.

"She's just trying to be nice." That was Grandma's voice. *"How would you feel if someone you were trying to be nice to was acting like you are?"*

I remembered how awful I felt when Sheila returned my note with those two short, icy sentences. That was the answer.

I would have to talk to Ruth during lunch, but after that, I would find a way to shake her. No one would notice me talking to her here, and I'd just make sure I didn't get stuck with her after this.

"Oh, down in all those flower streets," she was saying. "I live pretty far away from you."

I nearly said thank goodness, but of course I didn't.

"I take the bus to school. You walk, don't you?"

I nodded. I started on my apple. Ruth smelled of Noxema and her blouse was too tight. The middle button kept popping open and she kept giggling and blushing and closing it. Her face got all blotchy when she blushed. The other kids at the table didn't pay the slightest bit of attention to either of us.

"I never heard of a girl named Wallis before," Ruth said. "That's a really nice name. I hate the name Ruth. I wish I had a name like yours. Something distinguished. Ruth is so ordinary."

"Well, Wallis is *too* unusual for me," I said. "At least everyone knows you're a girl."

"Oh, I'd love to have an unusual name. You know what I always wished my name was?"

I shook my head.

"Glinda. Isn't that a beautiful name?"

Glinda, for heaven's sake. It figured.

"Isn't she the good witch in *The Wizard of Oz*?"

"That's right," said Ruth. "But I always thought it was a beautiful name anyway."

I didn't. I wouldn't want to be named Glinda any more than I want to be named Wallis. Maybe less.

"Ruth's okay," I said finally.

The bell rang. We dumped our trays and brought them to the tray table. Ruth started to follow me out of the lunchroom and I realized that there would be no getting rid of her before we got back to the classroom.

Suddenly a commotion erupted at a table right near the door, and a bunch of kids scrambled around trying to see what was going on.

Ruth rushed over to the table, calling for me to come too.

But I didn't. I ignored whatever the riot was about and slipped out the lunchroom door. I didn't know whether I could find my way back to room 203, but at least, if I ever got there, I wouldn't walk into it with Ruth hanging at my side.

F I V E

Stuffy stormed into the classroom looking outraged. Packy followed, with Sheila, Teddy, and B. G. right after them. The three girls were nearly doubled over with laughter. They staggered up the aisle to their seats.

"Did you see what happened?" Stuffy demanded, approaching my desk. I was so surprised that he was asking *me*, that I didn't say anything.

"That rotten Lemkin confiscated my worms."

I felt completely confused. For a minute I thought he was talking about a nasty dwarf, but then I realized Lemkin must be a teacher's name.

"She said they were disruptive."

Out of the corner of my eye I saw Ruth come in. She looked across the room at me questioningly and headed straight for my desk.

No! Don't talk to me! I wanted to shout.

Instead, I said to Stuffy quickly, too loudly, the first thing I could think of. "There's probably a rule about no fighting in the lunchroom."

Packy laughed and smacked Stuffy on the shoulder.

Stuffy looked so angry I was instantly sorry I had said it.

"Were they actually fighting?" I asked, trying to show how concerned I was, and at the same time, hoping that if I kept talking to Stuffy, Ruth wouldn't talk to *me*.

"I mean, after all this time," I went on stupidly, "if they *were* actually wrestling—"

Behind me I heard snickers. I didn't turn around. I didn't have to. Sheila, Teddy, and B. G. were cracking up at how stupid I was.

"She had no right to do that," Stuffy raged. "Those were my own personal, private property."

"Did she say she'd give them back?" I asked.

"Yeah. After school. But by that time they'll probably be dead. What does she know about taking care of worms?"

He vaulted over two desks to his own seat. Ruth plopped into the chair next to me and said, "Wallis, what happened to you? I looked all over for you but you just *disappeared*."

Everyone could hear her. Now, of course, everyone knew I'd been with her, even if they hadn't seen us.

"I came back here," I said shortly.

"I looked all over for you," she repeated, shaking her head.

Mr. Ryan came in and I breathed a sigh of relief as she went back to her own desk. I expected her to pack

———

up her looseleaf and her pencils and pen and move right next door to me, but she didn't.

In the afternoon we did some work. Most of it, Mr. Ryan said, was review of last year, but I listened very carefully, because it might not be review for me. Math was the major thing I was worried about, but it didn't seem like I was behind in it, since all the stuff we reviewed I at least recognized.

Finally the bell rang. I dawdled, gathering up all the books Mr. Ryan had handed out. I knew Ruth would have to go to catch her bus and if I waited long enough I wouldn't have to walk with her. Everyone else practically burst out of the room. Only Ruth said good-bye to me.

After she left I got up quickly, clutched the pile of books to my chest, and staggered out the door.

I was at the corner of Briar Lane when Stuffy and another boy came trotting after me.

"Hey, Wallis!" Stuffy yelled. "They're okay! They're fine!"

He dropped his books to the ground and took the little box from his pocket to show me Irving the Masked Marvel and Killer Krause.

"And you know what I thought of?" He bent down to pick up his books. "I thought if they were mating rather than fighting, more people might be interested in seeing them."

The other boy grinned. "And besides, you don't have to teach them how to mate."

"But if they're both boy worms—," I said uncertainly.

"Well, how do I know if they're both boys?" Stuffy said. We crossed the street. "Maybe they're not, and

---

maybe that's why they don't want to fight. Hey, Wallis, do you know how worms mate?"

It hadn't been that long ago since I'd learned how *people* mate, and I certainly didn't know the first thing about how worms did it. I shook my head.

"You're going to have to change their names," the other boy snickered.

"Oh, hey, Wallis, you know Eddie Bell? He's in our class too."

I said hi. I hadn't noticed him in class.

"Everybody calls him Ding Dong. Ding Dong Bell, get it?"

How original, I thought. But I didn't say it.

"He doesn't like that, though, so you call him Eddie. He's right, I'm going to have to change their names. I can't call them Killer Krause and Irving the Masked Marvel if they're not going to be wrestlers."

"Maybe you'd better look in the encyclopedia and find out how they mate first," I suggested. We were at the corner of Sweetpea Street. "I mean, it might not be something they'll just do for you any time you tell them."

"Besides," said Ding Dong, "who's going to come to Madison Square Garden to watch two worms mate?" He snorted.

"Maybe," Stuffy began excitedly, "we could have tag team matches! Two pairs of worms, and—"

"Tag team mating!" Ding Dong shouted. "You're crazy, man. They won't come to watch two worms mate, they won't come to watch *four* worms!"

"Perverts might," I said, trying to make Stuffy feel better.

"Hey," Stuffy said, "you know, if we say no one under

eighteen admitted, we ought to get them in by the thousands."

"X-rated worm shows!" Eddie howled. He dropped his books and they scattered all over the sidewalk. He was laughing so hard he couldn't pick them up.

"That's why you're going to be poor all your life, Bell," Stuffy said, "long after I'm rich and famous. You think small."

"*I* think small," Eddie cackled. He got down on his hands and knees and started collecting his books. "Ha ha."

"Well, I'll see you, Stafford," I said. "This is my block."

"Yeah, I know. Listen, think about new names for them, will you?"

"Maybe you ought to stick with the wrestling," I said gently. He certainly didn't seem to be pulling a big joke—and if he was, at least I knew it wasn't just a joke on *me*.

Of course, if it wasn't a joke, that made him a very weird person, but nobody else seemed to mind. And he was certainly interesting. And he was talking to me and walking me practically all the way home, just like a friend.

"And you can call me Stuffy," he said generously.

Grandma was ready to leave for Brooklyn when I got home. Her suitcase was in the back seat of the car. She and my mother had the screen door open and were nearly hanging out of it when I walked up the front steps. They both fired questions at once.

"OVERLOAD. OVERLOAD. CANNOT COMPUTE," I said. I dropped the books from my aching arms at the foot of the stairs.

47

"Don't drop your books on the floor," my mother said automatically. "Now, how was it?"

"Well . . ." I stopped to think. Parts of it were rotten, because everyone would lump me with Ruth Cutler if I weren't *very* careful and because Sheila, Teddy, and B. G. were not at all eager to be my friends, and because I was scared of Mr. Ryan and because I had felt awful for at least half the day, if not more.

But there was Stuffy, and I was not going to be way behind in the schoolwork and nobody had found out that I was living in the Tucker house and no one had called me Weird or made fun of my name, even though Mr. Ryan had harped on it so much. So there were some parts of the day that weren't so rotten.

I didn't know who I'd eat lunch with tomorrow, and I didn't know if I'd meet Stuffy on the way to school and I didn't know if I would make friends with any of the other kids in the class who I hadn't paid as much attention to as Sheila. I wasn't exactly looking forward to tomorrow, that was for sure. But at least today was behind me and I was still alive.

They were waiting for an answer. And since the day was not totally horrible, I finally said, "Okay."

They both smiled happily. "For you, Wallis," my mother reminded me, "that's practically good."

They really don't understand me.

SIX

My room was beginning to look like a souvenir shop.

Every night, my father brought home something from the city. The Empire State building, with a thermometer going up the tower; the Statue of Liberty with a clock in her stomach; a scarf with a street map of Manhattan silk-screened on it. He even got me a Yankee pennant for my wall. He said he did a lot of soul-searching before he bought that, because he had been a Brooklyn Dodgers fan in his youth, before the Dodgers moved to Los Angeles, and all Brooklyn Dodgers fans hated the Yankees.

As the first week of school came to a close, I wanted to tell him that there was no point in keeping up this campaign to make me love New York, because New York was where Briar Ane School was, and I really sympathized with the kid who wanted to get the L out of Briar Lane.

The way people ignored me, I could have been invisible. Except for Ruth, none of the girls in the class paid the littlest bit of attention to me. And it wasn't as if they hated me or anything—it was just that they all had their own friends and didn't even seem to know I was there. It was a very cliquey school. Everyone already had their own group of friends—or at least one friend—and didn't seem to want another one. Except Ruth.

Every lunch period was practically a replay of the first day. The only difference was Ruth tagged along with me from the classroom to the lunch line and I couldn't lose her without telling her right out to stop following me. So every day, instead of standing around in the middle of the room looking for a table by myself, I stood right up there, in plain sight of everyone, looking for a table with Ruth.

On Friday she led me to where Sheila, Teddy, and B. G. were eating. There were three spaces at the table and I was sure that Sheila would say they were saving the seats for someone, but Ruth didn't even ask. She sat right down with them, and I, wishing this wasn't happening, sat down next to her.

"Hi, Sheila," said Ruth eagerly. "Hi, Teddy. Hi, B. G." Like she hadn't just seen them all morning in class. Sheila only nodded. Teddy said, "Hi, Ruth. Hi, Wallis." B. G. went on eating her sandwich, staring right through Ruth as if she didn't exist.

The three girls were making plans to go roller-skating on Saturday and Ruth listened for a while. Then she broke into the conversation with a silly giggle. "I don't even know how to roller-skate," she said.

The three of them stared at her for a moment. Ruth began to get all red and blotchy as they fixed their eyes on her. Then B. G. went on with her sentence as if she'd never been interrupted.

I *did* know how to roller-skate. If only Sheila would say, "Hey, Wallis, want to come along?" But I knew she wouldn't. She wouldn't say anything to me as long as I was stuck with Ruth. And even if I weren't, why should they ask me?

Soon Ruth was jabbering away at me, like she did every day, and I was numbly eating my hamburger and giving her "Yes" and "No" answers. I wished she'd shut up. It was bad enough to have to be with her at all, but to be sitting here, with Sheila and her friends able to hear Ruth's stupid chatter, seeing me practically held *captive* by her was horrible. I was sure they were laughing to themselves about the two of us, and that later, when they were alone, they'd be in stitches, repeating all of Ruth's lunchtime talk.

Ruth was asking what my phone number was. "So I can call you," she said. "You could come over to my house tomorrow if you want."

I don't want! I want to go roller-skating with Sheila and Teddy and B. G. I want them to like me and they're never going to if you keep hanging onto me. How could I get out of this? How could I make them understand that I didn't want to be with Ruth, that they shouldn't lump me with Ruth, that I was not another Ruth-type person?

"I don't know," I lied. "I don't remember it."

"You don't know your own phone number?" Ruth said.

B. G. giggled and dug her elbow into Teddy's arm. Sheila stifled a laugh and looked across Teddy towards B. G. I felt so dumb and embarrassed I wanted to disappear. I didn't want them to think I was like Ruth and then I went and said something so Ruth-like that what else could they think?

"Wallis doesn't know her own phone number! Maybe they ought to give her a tag like the first graders wear on a class trip. MY NAME IS WALLIS. IF I GET LOST, CALL . . ."

I jumped up and snatched my tray, still full of food, from the table. I couldn't sit there anymore, couldn't eat, couldn't look at Sheila and B. G. exchanging snickers, couldn't stand the sight of Ruth's round, watery eyes. They reminded me of a puppy in the pound, waiting for someone to take him home.

"Wallis," Ruth called after me, "you didn't finish eating."

I ignored her. I dumped all the food from my tray and went back to room 203. I sat there, alone, until the bell rang.

In the afternoon Ruth said, "Don't forget, Wallis. You're coming to my house tomorrow."

"I didn't say I would, Ruth," Everyone was gathering up their books and sweaters and yelling, "T.G.I.F.!" No one was listening to us.

"I'll call you," she said. "I'll get your number from Information."

She ran to catch her bus.

No one said good-bye to me as I walked out of the room.

Mr. Ryan assigned social studies and math homework over the weekend. I didn't like him too much. He *was* sarcastic, though mostly with the boys who acted up, and he was very strict. But he didn't call on me if I didn't raise my hand and I hadn't raised my hand the whole week. So he hadn't said anything at all to me— just like everyone else in the class.

That first week Stuffy had walked home with me twice, but he didn't look for me or wait for me or anything like that. If we happened to run into each other, he and Ding Dong walked along with me to Sweetpea Street. If not, I walked alone. Everything might have been a little better if I could eat with Stuffy, but he was always at a table with boys, and boys and girls seemed pretty much to sit separately at lunch.

Friday afternoon I walked home by myself. The front door was unlocked and my mother had left a note saying she was shopping.

I went upstairs to my room, closed the door and dropped the books on my desk. I threw myself onto my bed, clutched a stuffed Snoopy I had had since the third grade, and cried.

All the tears saved up from the whole week flooded out of me. I relived every awful moment, from the first day to this morning's lunch, and each memory triggered a fresh burst of sobs. I thought I would never stop crying, but that was all right with me, because I never wanted to stop crying. I started to hiccup. My stomach began to hurt and my chest ached and my throat felt raw and tight, but it didn't matter. All those pains would go away. What wouldn't go away was the hurt that was making me cry in the first place. And that was the only hurt that counted.

* * *

Ruth called right in the middle of dinner. My mother answered the red phone on the kitchen wall and her face practically lit up when she said, "It's for you, Wallis."

She looked so happy, thinking I had a friend. But I knew who it was even before Ruth said, "Hello, Wallis? Are you coming tomorrow?"

"No, I can't." I would never go to Ruth's house. *Never.* If she was the only friend I could ever have at Briar Ane School, then I didn't want any friends at all.

"Why not?"

Why did she have to be so stubborn? *I* knew when I wasn't wanted. Why couldn't she tell that I didn't want to be her friend?

"I just can't. I have to do homework."

"We could do it together," Ruth said.

My parents were watching me, hanging on every word. My mother's face changed from happy to puzzled to disappointed. My father looked just plain sad.

"I can't. I'm eating now. I have to go. 'Bye."

I hung up and went back to the table.

"Who was that?" asked my father.

"A girl. From school."

I poked at the beets.

"Is she a friend of yours?" my mother asked.

"No! Definitely not! I don't have any friends. Especially not her."

"Oh, honey," my mother said, "how can you have any friends if you act like that?"

"No matter how I act I won't have any friends!"

"But you have one," my father said innocently. "That boy who told you about the Tucker murder."

"He's not my friend. He's just a kid I know. He has his own friends. Everybody has their own friends." Suddenly I was crying again.

"Well, this girl must have called you for a reason," said my mother. "I'm sure she would be your friend if you'd just let her."

"You don't understand!" I wailed. "You never understand. What do you know about it? I don't want to be friends with her."

"One friend leads to another," my mother said. "She knows people, and you get to meet them, and soon—"

"She doesn't have any other friends! That's why she keeps pestering *me*. And if I'm her friend, *I* won't have any other friends either."

"Well, if you don't have any now, what have you got to lose?" asked my father, trying to sound very calm and reasonable.

I pushed my plate away. I was crying too hard to eat.

"You complain that no one wants to be your friend and then when someone does, you treat them just the way you think people are treating you." My mother sounded very annoyed. "You of all people, Wallis, ought to understand how that girl feels. She probably feels just like you."

"She isn't like me!" I yelled. I jumped up from the table and ran out of the kitchen. "And I don't want to be like her!"

I dashed up the stairs and into my room. I slammed the door behind me.

I was furious. I was angry at them for every reason I had ever been angry before, and more. More dumb advice, more lectures; that was all I ever heard from them. If they knew what they were talking about, maybe their advice would do me some good, but they didn't. That didn't stop them, though. For all they knew Ruth could be a *drug pusher* or an *alcoholic* or something; they didn't know the first thing about her and they were urging me to be friends with her. They were so desperate for me to have a friend, any friend, that it didn't make a bit of difference to them what the friend was like.

I heard the phone ring again. A minute later there was a knock on my door. My mother opened it and said, "It's for you again, Wallis."

"If it's Ruth I don't want to talk to her."

"I think it's the same girl. And I want you to talk to her. I'm not going to tell her you won't come to the phone. And listen, Wallis. I understand how you feel—"

I snorted.

"Whether you think so or not," she went on firmly, "and no matter how unhappy you are, there's no excuse for being mean to someone else and making them unhappy. You're not making any effort to change things. You're not doing one thing to help yourself, and you're bringing most of your own troubles on yourself because of your attitude. All you have to do is try. That's all I'm asking. Even if you don't believe it, I hurt when I see you hurting. I want you to be happy, but I can't *make* you be happy. You have to do some work on that yourself."

"Being friends with Ruth is not going to make me happy," I said. "Exactly the opposite."

"I've never been able to make you do anything you don't want to do," she said. "You make your own choices."

Oh, sure. That was a laugh. What choices? Only the little ones. The big ones get made for me.

"Now don't keep that girl waiting on the phone any longer." She stood by the door until I went out of the room and into their bedroom to pick up the extension in there.

"Hi, Wallis. Are you finished eating?"

"Yeah. What is it?"

"Maybe you could come to my house Sunday. I mean, if you can't come Saturday." This girl never gave up. No matter how hard I pushed her away, she was going to keep springing back at me like a Popeye punching balloon I had when I was little. And suddenly, I was too tired to keep punching anymore.

I didn't care. I was worn out. Worn out by her stubbornness, and my parents' tight, disappointed faces, and by knowing that whether I went to her house or not, I was never going to go roller-skating with Sheila.

It didn't make any difference. Nothing made any difference. I would go to her house this one time, just to get my parents off the subject and off my back, and maybe she'd never ask me again. Especially when I didn't ask her to my house.

"I can come tomorrow," I said dully. "I'll do my homework tonight."

"Oh, that's great!" she bubbled. "Do you want my mother to come and pick you up?"

"No, my mother or father will drive me."

She gave me her address. "Do you know how to get here?"

"We have a town map from the Welcome Wagon lady. They'll find it."

"You want to come for lunch? You could stay for dinner, too. My mother said it's all right."

I could never stand her for that long. It was enough I had to eat lunch with Ruth every day, but two meals on Saturday was out of the question.

"No. I'll come after lunch and stay a little while." As little as possible, I thought.

"Okay. See you tomorrow." She sounded so excited at the thought of my visit that it made me feel a little sick. If she knew how I really felt about her, would she still sound so happy that she was spending the afternoon with me? Or wouldn't she care, just as long as I came?

I walked slowly out of my parents' bedroom, not even listening for the Ghost of Mr. Tucker. He hadn't shown up yet anyway—at least, not that I'd seen— while I had plenty of real, live problems to worry about. And no matter how hard I wished, my troubles would never, like ghosts, just pass through the wall and disappear.

SEVEN

My mother drove me to Ruth's the next day. She lived in what looked like a very expensive house on a very expensive block.

"They must be pretty well off," my mother commented.

"Money doesn't buy happiness," I reminded her. Ruth was a perfect example of that.

"Pick me up in an hour," I said, getting out of the car.

"Oh, Wallis, you can't stay just an hour!"

"Why not? I don't even want to stay five minutes!"

"Shh! Wait and see. If you don't want to stay after an hour, call me and I'll come and get you."

"Oh, all right," I sighed. I slammed the car door shut and started up the curving driveway to the house. I didn't want to walk across the lawn, which looked as if it had never been touched by human foot. Was this what my father was working so hard for? To have enough money so we could live in a house like this? So I could sit, like Ruth, like a princess in a castle complete with moat, and hope that someone would come and play with me?

My father's ambitions never seemed more pointless than at that very moment, when I stood at the gleaming, carved-wood front door and rapped the brass lion's-head door knocker.

Just as I knocked, I heard voices behind me on the street.

I turned around. There were Sheila, Teddy, and B.G., passing in front of Ruth's house. What awful timing! I didn't know if I should wave hello, or turn around quickly and hope that they hadn't recognized me. The door opened and Ruth practically threw herself on me.

"Wallis! Oh, I'm so glad you came!" She saw the three girls and waved violently.

"Hi, Sheila! Hi, Teddy! Hi, B. G.! Going skating?"

Sheila and B.G., who had their skates dangling over their shoulders, began to laugh. B.G. jabbed Sheila in the ribs and called back, "No, Ruth, we're going mountain climbing!"

Sheila gave a little whoop as if that was the funniest thing she'd ever heard. And after a moment, Ruth laughed, her silly, self-conscious giggle.

I hated them all. I hated Sheila and Teddy and B.G. for being so superior, stuck-up, and mean, and I hated Ruth for being Ruth, and for forcing me to come here and be humiliated again. I didn't want to be friends with *any* of them.

I followed Ruth into the house, sure that I could still hear Sheila and B.G. laughing at us. Ruth's mother,

Mrs. Cutler, made a big fuss over me, offering cake and milk and asking me all kinds of questions as if she were really interested in my life story.

She was so happy that someone had come to see Ruth that I think she would have given me Ruth's little sister, Lisa, if I'd asked for her. Lisa was seven, and so pretty it was hard to believe that she and Ruth were sisters. But Ruth didn't look much like her mother, either. Mrs. Cutler was slim and had auburn hair and not a popping button in sight.

Finally Ruth took me up to her room. It was filled with white French Provincial furniture, including a four-poster bed topped by a ruffled pink canopy. Ruth looked completely out of place there and I couldn't understand why. I kept thinking, I *can't picture her in this room*, even though she was sitting right in front of me on the plush pink rug. Then I remembered a magazine article I read about how to dress to look your best. It said that fat people should never wear ruffles. They should wear simple, tailored things with plain lines and avoid the frilly and fussy. That was it! Ruth's room should have been modern, neat, and uncluttered—it was dressed all wrong for Ruth.

"Do you want to play Monopoly?" Ruth asked.

Monopoly could take hours. I certainly didn't want to be here that long.

"No."

"How about cards? Do you know how to play Crazy Eights?"

"No."

"What do you want to do?" Ruth asked. She looked helpless.

I almost said, you're the one that made me come here. *You* think of something to do. But I didn't. I just shrugged.

"I know! I'll show you my scrapbooks!" Ruth's face brightened up. "You want to see my scrapbooks?"

That couldn't take too long. "Okay."

She opened the sliding door of the closet and bent down. When she straightened up and turned around, I saw an enormous pile of looseleaf notebooks stacked in her arms. My heart sank. I thought she meant one or two! There must have been eight notebooks in that pile. Monopoly would have taken less time than going through all those!

She sat down next to me on the rug and opened the first book.

"This is my dog scrapbook," she said. She started turning the pages. They were just regular, blue-lined looseleaf paper, with pictures of all kinds of dogs cut out of magazines and Scotch-taped on the pages. Underneath each picture she had written the breed of dog it was, except where she didn't know, and then she had put a question mark.

"I love dogs, don't you?" she said. "My mother won't let us have one because she says they're too messy. I wish I had a dog."

One by one she pointed out every picture, just as if I couldn't read the names for myself. "That's a collie. Don't you love collies? That's a poodle. They're the smartest dogs. My cousin has a poodle. Her name is Muffy. The poodle, I mean. She's practically human. She understands everything you say to her."

By the time Ruth finished showing me her dog scrapbook, I had turned into an animal hater. I loved dogs too, and wished I could have one, but now I didn't care if I saw another dog as long as I lived. I was thoroughly sick of dogs.

She reached for the next scrapbook. "This is Stars," she said. She had them labeled too, but this time there were no question marks.

"That's Robert Redford and that's Shaun Cassidy and that's Robert Redford and that's Burt Reynolds and that's Cher and that's Donny and Marie and that's John Denver and that's Kate Jackson . . ."

On and on she went. And when she finished with the movie star scrapbook, she picked up her interior decorating scrapbook. "This is all rooms I like," she explained. The rooms were labeled too, even the bathrooms and the kitchens. I mean, she just wrote, "BATHROOM" or "KITCHEN" or "BEDROOM" under each picture as if nobody would know what they were without the names written there.

I was dying of boredom. Somewhere in that house was a stack of cut-up magazines tall enough to reach the ceiling. It was incredible—and there were at least four more scrapbooks to go.

I couldn't stand it anymore. Halfway through her Horses scrapbook I interrupted her in the middle of a sentence about Shetland ponies and asked what time it was.

"Two-thirty," she said, glancing at the white clock-radio on her night table.

"Oh, boy, that late? I have to go."

"So soon? Oh, don't go. You haven't seen half of them yet. And I was saving the best one for last."

"No, I can't. I really have to go. Can I call my mother?"

Ruth sighed and closed the Horses book. She hauled herself up off the floor and led me into her parents' bedroom, where there was a gold phone right next to the bed. The whole huge room was gold and cream and the bedspread looked like satin. I didn't sit down on it. I was sure no one *ever* sat down on it.

"Mom? It's time for you to pick me up," I said into the phone. Ruth was listening to every word and I had to make it sound like it was my mother who'd told me when to come home.

"Wallis, you've hardly been there an hour." My mother's voice was pleading.

"Yeah, well, I'm on time, so you can come right over."

"All right," she said, sounding defeated. "I'm coming."

Ruth walked me downstairs and then, with her mother and Lisa, stood in the front hall with me waiting for my mother to come. Mrs. Cutler kept reminding me to come again, she was always happy to meet Ruth's friends—just as if Ruth had a whole bunch of friends who were always coming to the house. And she kept trying to make me eat something.

I thought my mother would never get there. We seemed to stand in the front hall for hours, the three of them hanging on me like they were afraid I'd escape. Lisa didn't say anything, but she kept staring at me, like I was an animal in the zoo. Maybe I was the first "friend" of Ruth's she had ever seen.

Finally my mother arrived and I tried not to run out the door and throw myself into the car. I remembered to say "thank you" to Mrs. Cutler and said good-bye to Ruth, who asked did I want to come again tomorrow?

I hadn't even gone yet and she was already pressing me about the next time I could come. Never, I vowed to myself. NEVER.

I still hadn't escaped. Mrs. Cutler and Ruth walked me out to the car, where Mrs. Cutler told my mother what a nice girl I was, and what a pleasure it was to have me come and visit. Either Mrs. Cutler was a big hypocrite or she hadn't noticed how rotten I'd acted. I didn't know how she could have missed it though. I knew I had not been a "nice girl" at all.

"Sweetpea Street? You don't, by any chance," Mrs. Cutler was asking my mother, "live in the house where that man was murdered?"

"Yes, that's right," said my mother. I wanted to scream. How could she do that to me? The whole week no one had found out where I lived, and now my mother had ruined everything.

Ruth gawked at me.

"How interesting!" Mrs. Cutler exclaimed. "A real conversation piece."

"That's what I think," my mother agreed. "It's so much more exciting to live in a place with a *history* behind it, than just an ordinary, run-of-the-mill house. I haven't managed to convince Wallis of that yet, though." She smiled at me. I could barely keep from snarling at her.

"Is it haunted?" asked Ruth, almost as if she was afraid to ask.

If it was haunted she wouldn't want to come and visit me. Of course, neither would anyone else. *Weird Wallis*. But no one else would come anyway. Ever.

"It might be," I hedged. "We don't know yet."

"For heaven's sake, Wallis!" My mother laughed. Mrs. Cutler was lauging too.

"Wouldn't that be something!" she said. "To have your very own ghost!"

"Well, we'll see if we can dig one up for you, Ruth, when you come to see us," my mother promised. Mrs. Cutler beamed. I seethed inside.

I clenched my fists together as we backed out of the long curved driveway and tried not to scream at her. How could she practically invite Ruth to come to the house without asking me first?

"You shouldn't have said that," I growled, when we pulled onto the street. "You have no right to do my inviting for me."

"They seem like very nice people," my mother said. "You were probably so convinced you wouldn't have a good time that you didn't even try. And I was embarrassed at the way you rushed out of there. As if you couldn't wait to get away."

"Well, I couldn't," I said angrily. "And I'll never go again. And I'll definitely never ask her over to our house."

My mother sighed. "That's up to you, Wallis. I can't force you."

"You keep saying that!" I shouted. "But you keep right on forcing me!"

She didn't say anything for a while, just kept her eyes fixed on the road. But when we got to a stoplight she turned toward me. I felt her looking at me, but I turned my head and stared out the window at a bunch of kids laughing and fooling around in front of somebody's driveway.

"I'm sorry," she said quietly. "I just wanted you to

give yourself a chance. I guess I did push you this time. I won't do it again."

The light turned green and she didn't say anything else the rest of the way home. Neither did I.

EIGHT

The next morning when my father went outside to bring in the Sunday papers from the front steps, he found Stuffy sitting on the bottom step. He came into the kitchen and told me there was a boy named Stafford W. Sternwood sitting there, waiting for me. He looked very pleased.

I jumped up, feeling pretty pleased myself, and went out to see what Stuffy wanted.

"Hi, Stuffy. My father told me you were here."

"Hi, Wallis. Listen, can you type?"

"Type? Like with a typewriter? No, not really. I can find the letters, though, and if I go real slow I guess I could type something. Why?"

His eyes gleamed, almost sending little sparks of light through his glasses.

"I had this really great idea and I need help with it. How are you at writing?"

"I think I have a nice handwriting. Neat, anyway."

"No, that's not what I mean. Can you write, you know, stories, stuff like that?"

"Oh. Yeah, I guess so. I'm pretty good at that. Why? What's your great idea?"

He looked around carefully, as if to make sure that no one was listening, then lowered his voice. "You know what would be funny? What if Ruth the Doof started getting love letters from Mr. Ryan?"

"Ruth the Doof?" Is that what they called her? It was the first I'd heard of it. But it figured.

"Yeah. Can you just picture her getting this really *steamy* letter telling her that Mr. Ryan can't live without her?"

I began to giggle. I could picture it. I could see Ruth's face getting all red and her pale little eyes opening so wide they nearly popped out of her head.

"And then when she comes into school the next day? I can't wait to see how she acts after she gets the letter," he went on, grinning wickedly. He clasped his arms around his stomach as if to hold the laughter in.

"It sounds like a mean trick," I said. But I giggled again. I couldn't help it.

"Not that mean. We'll be the only ones who'll know."

I thought of yesterday afternoon at Ruth's. I remembered her embarrassing me in front of Sheila, Teddy, and B. G. I remembered her silly comments at lunch. I hated her for being persistent and boring and acting as if she was my friend in front of everybody. I hated her for following me around like a dog and making sure that no one would be friends with me because *she* was trying to be friends with me.

The idea of playing a trick—even a mean trick—on Ruth was very appealing. And Stuffy had asked me to help him. No one would know but us. We would be sharing a secret. Just like friends.

I imagined him exchanging knowing glances with me every morning when Ruth came into class. I pictured us smothering our laughter behind our hands, cracking up over our private secret. I thought of how it would feel to share that kind of laughter with someone, instead of being the one who was snickered at.

And Stuffy wanted *me* to help him. Of all the kids he could have asked, he asked me. He wanted to be my friend. *"You have to be a friend to make a friend."* Being a friend means helping someone when they need you.

"I'll do it!"

"Great!" He grabbed my hand and pumped it hard. "Let's go. We'll use my mother's typewriter."

I yelled in to my parents to tell them I was going to Stuffy's.

Stuffy was so excited about the joke that we jogged all the way to his house and were breathless by the time we got there.

Stuffy mumbled an introduction to his parents and his older sister, Jean, and took me into the den. There was a typewriter on the desk, but Stuffy reached into a drawer for pencil and paper.

"We'll do a rough copy first and then type it out," he said. "If we mail it today, she might get it tomorrow, but probably not till Tuesday."

"Do you think anyone types love letters?" I asked. "Don't you think she'll be suspicious?"

"Nah. Once she sees what's in the letter she'll be too—too—"

"Flabbergasted?" I suggested.

"Thank you. Flabbergasted to think about the typing. Now—" He tapped the pencil thoughtfully against his front teeth. "Dear Ruth. Dear Ruth."

"'Dearest Ruth,'" I said. "No, wait, 'My dearest Ruth.'"

"Good! Good!" He scribbled it down. "'My dearest Ruth. Ever since the first day I saw you . . . Ever since the first day I saw you' what?"

I thought a minute. "'Ever since the first day I saw you . . . my heart has not been my own.'"

"Nah. That sounds like he rented it out to someone."

"No it doesn't. Well, maybe I can think of something better."

We sat in silence for a moment.

"This is even harder than I thought," said Stuffy.

"We'll get it. We just have to get started, then it'll all come at once. Let's see. 'Ever since the first day I saw you—' wait—'I have been fighting to . . . to . . .' No! 'I have been fighting an overwhelming urge to take you in my arms—'"

"Slow down! Slow down!" Stuffy was scrawling furiously. "Fantastic!" He cackled wildly. "How do you spell *overwhelming?*"

"O-v-e-r-w—oh, we'll look it up later. Hurry and get it down before I forget it."

"I got it. 'Urge to take you in my arms.'"

"Okay. Period. 'Every day that I see you, I . . .'"

"What?" Stuffy stopped writing.

"I don't know. Let me think." I rested my chin in my hand while Stuffy drummed the pencil against the desk.

"'Every day I see you I love you more'?" he said.

"No. Make it mushier. 'Every day I see you . . . I am overcome by your beauty—'"

"Aw, she'll never believe that!" Stuffy jeered.

"Well, if she believes this letter at all," I retorted, "she'll believe that he thinks she's beautiful. But I'll think of something else. 'Every day I see you . . . the urge gets stronger.'"

"Good!" Stuffy wrote it down. "Keep going."

Now the words were coming to me faster than I could say them.

"'I no longer know how long I can fight or if I can ever overcome the—the—passion exploding within me.'"

"Beautiful!" Stuffy howled. "How do you spell *passion?*"

"I don't know. Look it up later. 'But because of the difference in our ages, I must keep this love a secret and so must you.'"

"Difference with an 'a-n-c-e' or an 'e-n-c-e'?" asked Stuffy.

"Just write!" I yelled. "Don't worry about spelling now!"

"Okay, okay. Keep going. It's magnificent."

"Thank you," I nodded. "'It will have to be enough to see you every morning and to dream about you every night—'"

"Ohhh!" Stuffy flung himself off the chair and onto the floor, clutching the paper to his heart. "Ohh, this is genius! Sheer genius!"

"Write!" I ordered. "'It will have to be enough to see you every morning and dream of you every night. Though I can never take you in my arms and tell you

---

all the things you are to me . . .' Oh, darn, now I've lost it."

"That's all right. Take your time. I'll come back to you." Stuffy waited, his face all eager and expectant.

I rubbed my forehead, as if that would help push the words out.

"Where was I?"

" 'Though I can never take you in my arms and tell you all the things you are to me . . . ,' " he read back.

"Oh. Okay. Um . . . 'at least I will see you every day and know that you know what is in my heart.' I don't like that last part too much," I added.

"It's good, it's good," Stuffy insisted.

"Oh, all right, leave it in then. 'We must never talk of this. Our love must remain a secret which we will carry to our grave.' "

"Oh," moaned Stuffy, "that's heartbreakin'." He pretended to wipe away a tear.

"And then I think we should just end it. How about, 'Your adoring secret lover'?"

"No." Stuffy shook his head. "Sounds funny. How about just, 'Your secret lover'?"

"No. Not flowery enough. Anyway we're going to sign it, aren't we? He won't be a secret."

"But that he loves her is the secret," Stuffy pointed out.

"Well, let's see. Gee, this is the hardest part. I can't think of anything that sounds right after all that goo."

"Yeah. I know what you mean. You can't just put 'Yours truly.' "

"Think," I ordered myself. "*Think.*"

"I've got it!" said Stuffy. His face lit up with sudden inspiration. " 'Your beloved till the End of Time!' "

"Hey, that's beautiful!" I said. "That's absolutely beautiful. I didn't know you had it in you, Stuffy."

"Thank you," he said modestly. He wrote it down.

"Stuffy! Do you know Mr. Ryan's first name? We can't sign a letter like that 'Mr. Ryan.'"

"Yeah, don't worry. It's James."

"Oh, good," I said, relieved.

"What should we do about signing it?" asked Stuffy. "Can you copy Mr. Ryan's signature?"

"I've never seen Mr. Ryan's signature. Besides, wouldn't that be forgery?" The whole letter was a forgery, but I didn't want to think about that now.

"We'll have to type it then," said Stuffy. "She'll never notice."

"Let's read it back and see how it sounds." He read it out loud and I listened carefully. I thought it sounded terrific.

"I do too," said Stuffy. "Let's get it typed up and mail it right away."

We looked up "overwhelming" and "passion" in the dictionary. Then I sat down at the desk and Stuffy gave me a piece of typing paper. I rolled it into the typewriter and started, very slowly and carefully, to type as he read the letter to me again.

It seemed to take forever. I tore out three sheets of paper because I had made mistakes, and then decided I'd just have to X out the mistakes or we'd never get it done. When it was finally finished, I was exhausted.

I pulled it out of the typewriter and looked at it.

My dearest Ruth,
Ever since the first day I saw you I have
been fighting an overwhelming urge to take

_____

you in my arms. every day I see uou the urge
gets stronger. I no longer xx know how long
I can fight or if i can ever overcome the
passion exploding with in me. but because
of the xx diffexrence in our ages I must
keep this love a secret and so must you. It
will have to be enough to see you every
morning and to dream bout xxx you every
night. Though I can never take you in my
Arms and tell you all the things you are to
me at least I will see you every day and
know that you kow what is in my xxxx heart.
We must never talk of this. our love must
remain a secret wich we will carry to our
grave. Your beloved till the Endo of time.

James Ryan.

"Gee, Stuffy, it really doesn't look too good," I said.
"I don't know if she'll believe this came from Mr. Ryan."

"Once she starts reading it she'll never notice how it
looks," Stuffy said. "Don't worry. Now the envelope."

Stuffy started to look up Ruth's address in the phone
book, and without thinking, I told him what it was.

"How did you know?" he asked.

"Well—she—uh, she told me," I said, confused. I
didn't want to mention that I had been at her house
yesterday.

"Why'd she tell you?"

"Well . . . she kind of forced me to come over," I
admitted.

Stuffy looked at me curiously. "She's not your *friend*,
is she?"

"Of course not! I wouldn't play this trick on her if she was my friend, would I?"

"Then why'd you go to her house?"

"My mother made me. She wants me to make friends. I didn't want to go. And I had a really crummy time."

"Oh. Okay."

"And I'll never go again," I swore.

"All right. I was just wondering."

I typed up the envelope carefully. The address came out kind of low and over to one side on the front, but we left it that way. At least I didn't make any typing mistakes on it, and that was the important thing. Stuffy found a stamp in the desk drawer and stuck it on the letter.

"There's a mailbox on the next block," he said. "Let's go mail it right now."

Neither of us could stop giggling as we raced to the mailbox. Stuffy opened the lid and I dropped the letter in.

"There!" he said, letting the lid slam shut. "Now all we have to do is wait." He read the little schedule on the lid. "She might get it tomorrow. They pick up the mail at two-fifteen on Sundays."

"I can't wait to see her face!" I said.

"Yeah! And when she tries to look at him—"

"And when he calls on her!"

"Ohh, boy!" Stuffy rolled his eyes back in his head. "But listen," he said, suddenly serious, "you won't tell anyone about this, will you?"

"Of course not! I wouldn't tell anyone no matter what!"

"Good. Neither will I." He held out his hand and I shook it.

Stuffy went back to his house and I started for home.

Somehow, now that the letter was mailed, I had a sort of let-down feeling. The joke didn't seem as funny as it did at first.

Well, I guess the really funny part would come after Ruth got the letter. For now, we just had to wait. And the main thing was that Stuffy and I had a Sworn Secret. We were in this together, like friends. Friends to The End.

Or—I thought suddenly—partners in crime.

NINE

Ruth blabbed.

I knew she would.

Maybe if she had gotten the letter Monday morning, she would have been too overcome with passion to even remember that I lived in the Tucker house, let alone tell the whole school by lunchtime.

But I could tell the minute she walked into class that she hadn't gotten the letter yet. Stuffy turned around to catch my eye. He was two seats in front of me, in the row next to mine. "Tomorrow," he mouthed. I nodded and clamped my lips together to keep from laughing.

I thought I had solved the problem of eating with Ruth by bringing my lunch from home instead of buying it. That way, she would have to wait in line and

I would find a spot at a table before she was ready to sit down.

That part worked out fine. I found a seat right away, next to a girl in my class who I had hardly noticed last week. Her name was Bonnie Trask. The only reason I knew her name was because Mr. Ryan called on her so much. She wasn't the kind of girl who was always waving her hand in the air, practically dying to be called on. She would look around, hesitating, and when she was sure no one else could answer the question, she would slowly raise her hand. She was very smart, I guess, because she always gave the right answer.

Bonnie always came into class with a girl named Lynn. I figured Lynn was Bonnie's best friend, but she wasn't at the table. I tried to remember if she'd been in class that morning, but I didn't even know where she sat. All I knew about Lynn was that she giggled a lot.

I sat down opposite Bonnie at the table. There were still a couple of empty spaces there. I hoped they would fill up before Ruth got her lunch and found me.

"Can I sit here?" I asked. I was already sitting.

"Sure," said Bonnie. She unwrapped a sandwich. "You're new here, aren't you?"

"Yeah. We just moved in a couple of weeks ago."

"I've only been here a year myself. How do you like it?"

"Well . . ."

"I know what you mean. It's not so bad, though, once you get used to it. Where did you move from?"

She had a nice face. Short, straight hair, almost black, and fair skin. And she seemed really interested in me.

"You name it," I said, trying to joke about it, "and I've moved from there. San Francisco, Denver, Indianapolis, and Philadelphia."

"Wow, you've been all over the country," she said. She bit into her sandwich. "We only moved here from Brooklyn."

"My grandmother lives in Brooklyn. Maybe you know her."

Bonnie grinned. "Brooklyn's a big place. What's her name?"

"Mae Greene."

Bonnie thought a moment, then shook her head. "No, I don't think so."

I was just beginning to feel a little comfortable with Bonnie when Lynn clattered her tray onto the table next to her and sat down across from me.

The first thing she did was giggle. "Salisbury steak," she said, pointing to her plate. She didn't even look at me.

I didn't think Salisbury steak was so funny. I guess Bonnie didn't either, because she just looked puzzled.

"Packy said they ground up all the sneakers from Lost and Found and put them in with the meat and made the gravy with turpentine." She giggled again. "Isn't that funny?"

"It depends on whether you have to eat that or not," Bonnie said. "You know Wallis," she added. "She's in our class."

Lynn noticed me for the first time.

"Oh, hi," she said. "I wanted to ask you about your name all week."

Then why didn't you, I wondered? Even though I'm tired of explaining it, it would have been better to explain it a couple of more times than to be ignored.

"My grand—," I started, then caught myself. No use making it more complicated than it had to be. "*They* named me after a duchess. See, there was this American woman who married the King of England and he gave up his throne for her and her name was Wallis. That's where they got the name."

"How romantic!" Lynn said. "I never heard a name like that before. Not for a girl."

"Well, you spell it with an *I-S*," I said. "Not like the boy. That's *A-C-E*."

I suddenly realized I had practically eaten my whole sandwich and I didn't even know what kind of a sandwich it was. Lynn and Bonnie were *interested* in me. They thought *I* was interesting. They didn't think my name was weird at all. And maybe the reason they hadn't talked to me the whole week was because I hadn't talked to *them*. "*You have to be a friend to make a friend.*"

I began on my apple. I was feeling almost happy. For the first time since I had set foot in the lunchroom of Briar Ane School, I felt like a part of things.

"Uh oh," said Lynn. "Look what's coming."

I turned around. Marching toward me, led by Sheila, were Teddy, B. G., and Ruth. They were heading right for this table, and for a moment, I couldn't imagine what they wanted. They couldn't have anything to say to *me*.

"Wonder why Ruth the Doof is tagging along?" Lynn said.

"Shh!" hissed Bonnie. But she giggled. She couldn't help it either. And she seemed like a nice person. Not even the nicest person could like Ruth, I thought.

"Wallis," Sheila said, "is it true?"

———

"Is what true?" But suddenly, I knew. One look at Ruth's flushed face, and I knew.

"Do you live in the Tucker house?"

"*Be proud,*" I heard my mother saying. "*Well, maybe proud isn't the right word. . . .*"

Now I was more worried about what Bonnie would think than how Sheila would react. After all, Sheila had seen me at Ruth's house Saturday and there was no chance that she'd ever be friends with someone she thought was friends with Ruth. But Bonnie was listening and I didn't want to say the wrong thing now, just when someone seemed to like me a little.

"Yeah, that's right."

"Where that woman murdered her husband?" Sheila went on.

"Yup. Right in my parents' bedroom. Of course, it wasn't my parents' bedroom then, it was the Tuckers' bedroom."

I thought I was doing pretty well so far. I glanced at Lynn. Her eyes were as wide as Ruth's had been on Saturday. Her mouth was hanging open too. Bonnie just looked extremely curious.

"Why didn't you tell us?" B. G. demanded.

I looked at her blankly. "You didn't ask me."

Suddenly I realized that they weren't going to make fun of me. They were *fascinated.* In fact, instead of not wanting to ever come to my house because of possible haunting, I had a feeling they were dying for me to invite them. There was six girls, hanging on my every word, looking at me as if I owned Disney World. Nothing like this had ever happened to me before. Was my mother right? Was Grandma right? Was my own attitude the important thing?

Or was I just lucky enough to land in a school that was completely populated by murder freaks?

"Honestly, Wallis," Sheila began, looking irritated, "the Tucker murder was just about the biggest news this town ever saw."

"How was she supposed to know that?" asked Bonnie quietly. "She just moved here."

"Aren't you scared?" asked Lynn. "I mean, isn't it scary knowing that a bloody murder happened right there in your own parents' bedroom?"

"Well—" I hesitated. I wasn't really sure how to answer that. Did they want to believe there was something scary about the house? Or would they think I was a big coward if I said I was scared? *"Wallis sleeps with a night-light."* I decided to tell the truth. They certainly didn't seem to be looking for something to tease me about.

"Actually, when I first found out, it was pretty scary. After all, my bedroom is right next to my parents'. I mean, there I was, lying in bed in the dark, knowing that only a few feet away, a grisly crime had left blood spattered on the walls."

My, that was good! I was warming up to the story. All six girls stared, wide-eyed and fascinated . . . especially during that part about the blood spattered on the walls. I must admit, that sounded terrific.

"Was there really blood on the walls?" gasped Teddy. She made a face, as if that was too horrible to think about. Maybe it was. Better not dwell on it.

"Oh, no, not by the time we moved in. I guess they cleaned it up pretty well. At least, we can't *see* any blood. But I saw this movie once and they said you could never completely wash away the traces of human blood. Even though you might not see it with the naked eye, it's still there."

I looked around. They were eager for more details. No one said a word. They just waited for me to go on.

"Anyway, there I was, the first night. My room was *completely black*. And I heard creaking on the stairs."

All six girls leaned forward. Lynn nearly fell into her Salisbury steak.

"But it was just my parents coming up to bed."

They all breathed out at once. It was like a small gale blowing past our table. They were relieved, but they looked disappointed.

"Then my parents went to bed. And my grandmother—she was visiting—went to bed. All the lights upstairs went off. It was quiet. For a few minutes."

They sensed something more coming. No one breathed. Suddenly Teddy blurted out, "Weren't your parents scared to sleep in that room?"

"Shhh!" Five people turned to her angrily. "Be quiet." They turned back to me. "Go on, Wallis."

"There was a moon," I continued dreamily. My voice got very soft. They had to lean even further forward to hear me. I had never had such a wonderful time in my whole life. Not even on birthdays.

"The moon made shadows in my room. At least, I *think* they were shadows. I'm not sure."

Ruth gave a little whimper of fear, almost as if she were living through the whole thing herself at that very moment.

"*Shhh!*"

"Well, of course, by this time I was a little nervous."

"A little nervous!" B. G. cried. "A *little* nervous!"

———

"But I thought, maybe my imagination is running away with me. Maybe that shadow in the corner was only . . . a shadow. Well, to tell you the truth, I was just about to pull the covers over my head so I wouldn't see . . . anything . . ."

Lynn shuddered. The other girls nodded, as if they knew just how scared I was. They didn't seem to think it was weird to want to hide under the covers in a situation like that. I realized that they didn't think being scared was cowardly—they thought it was normal. That was just the way any of them would have felt.

"So I'm about to pull the covers up over my head when I hear . . . a creaking on the stairs again. *Only this time there was nobody there.*"

"Ohhh."

I scrunched up my lunch bag. Six pairs of eyes were still gazing at me. I looked from one face to another. Did they want more? But there wasn't any more. That was all.

"Then what happened?" demanded Sheila.

I thought for a moment. Finally I just shrugged. "Whatever It was," I said mysteriously, "It didn't come into *my* room."

"Did It go into your parents' room?" asked Bonnie.

"They didn't tell me It did. But they might not want to scare me, so even if something did happen, they probably wouldn't tell me. I didn't even know until after we moved in that there was anything . . . strange about the place."

"Well, are they acting funny? Jumpy or anything?" asked B. G.

"As a matter of fact," I said, telling the *absolute* truth,

"my father is getting these dark circles under his eyes. I mean, like really big, dark circles."

"Like he's lying awake all night," breathed Teddy, "waiting."

I nodded. He wasn't getting enough sleep, that was for sure. But that was probably because he had to get up at six o'clock every morning and hated to go to bed before I did. And because he was working so hard that he was always tired.

The bell rang.

I got up to dump my bag in the metal can. Bonnie, Lynn, and Ruth followed me.

"Do you believe in ghosts?" Bonnie asked doubtfully. "Do you think the ghost of the murdered man is hanging around your house?"

"I don't know," I said. "I never did believe in ghosts before we moved here."

"Why didn't you tell me?" Ruth asked, her face almost white. "Why didn't you tell me there was a ghost when—"

I broke in so she couldn't finish the sentence with "when you were at my house Saturday."

"I didn't know you were interested," I lied. I turned briskly and walked off, leaving her standing in front of the trash can.

At three o'clock I was still feeling so good about what had happened at lunch that I went over to Bonnie as she was collecting her books and asked her where she lived. I thought maybe I could walk home with her.

"Cardinal Avenue," she said. "You know where the bird streets are?"

I shook my head. "No. But we nearly bought a house on Titwillow Way."

She smiled. "You're down in the flower streets, right? That's the opposite direction from me."

"Oh." I tried not to sound disappointed. Lynn stood with her jacket and her books at the door. "Come *on*, Bonnie."

"Well. See you," I said.

"Yeah. See you tomorrow."

Okay. So I couldn't walk home with her. But this time, instead of hoping that Stuffy would call to me on the street, I ran down the stairs and out into the schoolyard and looked for *him*. After all, we were still sharing a secret. We were friends. I spotted him a little way down the street, walking with Ding Dong.

"Hey, Stuffy!" I yelled. "Wait a minute!"

He turned around and waved and waited for me to catch up to him.

"She didn't get it," I muttered under my breath, meaning Ruth and the letter. I really didn't know what else to say. I just wanted to walk home with him.

"I know," he said, without moving his lips. "Tomorrow."

"Who didn't get what?" Ding Dong asked. I hadn't thought he'd hear us. "And what's tomorrow?"

Stuffy and I exchanged nervous glances.

"The joke," Stuffy said hastily. "She didn't get the joke."

"What joke? Who didn't get it?"

Stuffy looked frantic for a minute.

"My mother," I said, thinking fast. "Stuffy told me a joke and I told it to her and she didn't get it."

"What's the joke?" Eddie demanded.

Stuffy's eyes went blank. I knew he was desperately racking his brain for a joke to tell Eddie. Suddenly he nodded, as if he had just found what he was looking for.

'Uh, well there was this guy who went to a train station and he asked the ticket seller for a round trip ticket. And the ticket seller said, 'To where?' and the guy said, 'To here.'"

Eddie didn't say anything for a minute. Then he shook his head.

"I don't get it."

"Neither did my mother," I said.

"A round trip ticket," Stuffy repeated. He made a circle in the air with his finger. "*Round* trip."

"I still don't get it. And what's tomorrow?"

"Tuesday," Stuffy said cheerfully.

Eddie looked absolutely bewildered by now. He just kept shaking his head. Stuffy winked at me—at least, he tried to wink, I think, but both eyes closed.

"What was all that about at lunch?" Stuffy asked suddenly. "It looked like you were surrounded."

"Oh, that." I smiled, remembering my few moments of glory. "You-know-who told Sheila about where I live. They wanted to hear all the gory details."

"Who's you-know-who?" asked Ding Dong.

"It's funny," I said. "I think they really wanted to hear that the place was haunted."

"Yeah?" Stuffy said thoughtfully.

"I had this feeling they were dying to see the scene of the crime."

"Yeah?" Stuffy said again. I looked over at him. The wheels were turning in his brain. I could tell. I didn't know what he was thinking, but I knew he was working on *something*.

"What crime?" asked Eddie. "Who's you-know-who?"

"The Tucker murder," Stuffy said impatiently. "In Wallis' house."

"Oh, that crime." Eddie made it sound like Crestwood was such a hotbed of violence that you couldn't keep track of the murders without a scorecard.

"Is it haunted?" he asked.

"Well, actually—," I began.

"Wallis doesn't know for sure," Stuffy cut in loudly.

We'd reached the corner of Sweetpea Street and I stopped to look at him. I was puzzled. Why hadn't he let me finish the sentence?

"As a matter of fact," I began again.

"You never can tell," Stuffy interrupted, staring hard at me. "*Right, Wallis?*"

Stuffy was so insistent that I not tell Eddie if the house was haunted that I felt confused. So I just shrugged and said, "I guess," weakly.

"See you later," Stuffy said as I turned down the street. He sounded almost eager to get rid of me, as if he didn't want me to have a chance to say another word to Ding Dong.

I walked down Sweetpea Street slowly, wondering what that had been all about. For some reason, Stuffy wanted to let Eddie think that there might be a ghost living in my house. But what was the reason?

What in the world was going through Stuffy's mind?

T E N

I couldn't wait to get to school Tuesday.

Ruth would surely have gotten the letter by now and I was dying to see her face when she walked into class. I actually left ten minutes early to make sure I would be in the room when she came in.

My mother couldn't believe how anxious I was to get to school.

I'd called Grandma Monday night and told her all about the girls at lunch, and how they'd acted when I described the night I found out about the murder. I told my mother all about it too. They both said, "You see? What did I tell you? Your own attitude is the important thing."

Even so, my mother was a little rattled when I bolted down breakfast and raced out of the house with a cheery "See you!"

In fact, so was I. I practically bounced up Sweetpea Street, and it was so strange to feel that spring in my step that I could almost feel myself watching myself bounce.

Am I really this happy, I wondered? Am I really looking forward that much to getting to Briar Ane School that I would be *skipping* up the street if I wasn't too old to skip? Can this really be *me*?

As if I was a perfect stranger, I stood back in my mind and watched Wallis Greene hurry to school. There goes a happy girl, I told myself. There goes a girl with a bright future. There goes a girl who thinks things are finally going to work out.

"There goes a girl who is cracking up," I muttered, and burst into a fit of giggles.

I didn't see Stuffy on the way to school, and I hoped he would get there before Ruth did. It wouldn't be half as much fun if I didn't get to share Ruth's entrance with him. In fact, it wouldn't be any fun at all.

Only one school bus had arrived by the time I got to school, and I hoped it wasn't Ruth's. I went right up to Room 203. She wasn't in her seat yet, so I was in time. Mr. Ryan was writing on the chalkboard.

"Hi, Mr. Ryan," I said cheerfully. He looked almost startled.

"Good morning, Wallis."

For one wild moment I pictured him clutching Ruth in his arms and murmuring passionate words into her frizzy hair. I whirled around and dashed to my seat, before I had hysterics right there in front of him.

A moment later Stuffy came charging into the room, huffing like a steam engine with asthma. He looked around quickly, just as I had, and slumped against the door to catch his breath.

***

Mr. Ryan turned to look at him.

"Morning," gasped Stuffy.

"Are you all right?"

"Great, great," Stuffy wheezed.

"I never knew you were this eager for education," Mr. Ryan said with a little smile.

"It's not that," Stuffy panted. "I took the stairs too fast."

"I should have known," Mr. Ryan muttered. He turned back to the chalkboard.

Stuffy limped over to my desk and sat down next to me. My seat partner, a boy named Arthur Deegan, who never said a word to me or anyone else, wasn't there yet.

"I ran all the way," Stuffy whispered. "The buses were just coming in when I got here. Any minute now."

Sure enough, the noise level in the halls started to build and our empty classroom began to come to life. Bonnie and Lynn came in. I smiled and waved to them as they took their seats, and Lynn actually called, "Hiya, Wallis!" as she sat down. Bonnie gave me a nice warm smile and went to hang up her sweater.

I would definitely eat with them today, I decided. My lunch problem was solved. I was sure Bonnie would never say, "This seat is saved," if I sat down next to her, and Lynn was so interested in the murder at my house that she'd be glad to hear more—if only there was something more to tell.

That reminded me of Stuffy's strange behavior yesterday with Eddie.

"Hey, Stuffy, I meant to ask you," I began, "why didn't you want me to tell Ding Dong that—"

"*Shh!* Here she comes!"

And there she was, trailing behind Sheila, Teddy and B. G. B. G. was giggling and rolling her eyes. Ruth stepped into the room, not at all like her usual lumbering self, but like a person tiptoeing over eggs in a dense fog.

She was wearing a dress. It was pale pink and sort of silky looking, with a ruffle going around the bottom of it, and long, filmy white sleeves. She was dressed as wrong as her room was.

Stuffy jabbed me so hard in the ribs that I gasped.

"She got it," he choked, and held onto the edge of the desk like it was a life preserver and if he let go he'd drown.

She had to pass Mr. Ryan at the chalkboard to get to her desk. She stopped to look at him, then began to blush furiously. She looked quickly down at the floor, like there might be bear traps ready to spring.

Slowly, carefully, she drifted down the row to her seat, her eyes now staring at the back of the room, not seeing anything, not looking at anyone, just staring.

"She's in a daze," whispered Stuffy. "Look at her, she's in a *daze*."

"Hey, Ruth," called B. G., "how come you're so dressed up?"

At the sound of her name Ruth seemed to snap out of it. Her eyes cleared and focused on B. G. But there was a look of confusion about her, and embarrassment. No one dressed like that for school; even Ruth the Doof knew that.

"Oh," she said finally, her voice squeaky, "I thought it would be nice for a change." She flopped into her seat and began fiddling with her pencils.

Stuffy jabbed me with his elbow again. This time I jabbed back.

"Told you she'd fall for it," he muttered, covering his mouth with his hand.

Arthur Deegan was standing patiently next to his desk, waiting for Stuffy to get out of the seat so he could sit down.

"Watch her when he calls the roll," Stuffy advised. He jumped up and made a gallant bow to Arthur, gesturing for him to take the seat. Arthur just nodded and sat down.

Unfortunately, Ruth was sitting in front of me, so when Mr. Ryan called her name, I couldn't see her face. Stuffy could, though, because he was sitting one row across from her. He turned to look at me, his lips pressed tightly together. He tried to wink, and both eyes closed again. But I got the idea.

Ruth had said "Here" so softly I hadn't even heard her.

Yet, I don't know why . . . Somehow it wasn't as much fun as I'd imagined it would be. First of all, I couldn't see Ruth's face, so through most of the rest of the morning, I had no idea how she was reacting to Mr. Ryan. Second of all, watching somebody being self-conscious just wasn't that funny. Maybe I had been self-conscious too many times myself to get a kick out of someone else's embarrassment, but whatever the reason was, the whole thing wasn't turning out like I'd expected.

Every once in a while, Stuffy would swivel around in his seat to roll his eyes or wink at me through his glasses. I'd nod, and try to grin as if I was really appreciating the joke. Once, after one of his two-eyed winks, I winked back at him. He scowled and looked frustrated, and didn't try to wink at me after that. I can do a one-eyed wink, because I practiced for four days once in the third grade, in front of a mirror, until I was able to hold one eye open.

Just before lunch, Mr. Ryan called on Ruth to do a math problem at the chalkboard. It was multiplying fractions. I looked over at Stuffy as Ruth walked slowly to the board. He had his hand clamped over his mouth like he was afraid he'd throw up.

Ruth started to do the problem. The first thing she did was to turn the second fraction upside down, which you only have to do when you divide fractions.

"No, Ruth, multiply, not divide." She got all flustered and erased the second fraction. Then she stood there, with the eraser in one hand and the chalk in the other, looking helpless. She turned to Mr. Ryan in desperation.

"I forget what the other fraction is," she said.

"Four ninths," he said gently.

She seemed to melt. As if she forgot she was in a class full of people who usually made fun of her, she just gazed at him with adoring eyes, like he was the only person in the room.

"Four ninths," he repeated. He actually looked a little uncomfortable.

A couple of people giggled. Stuffy was turning bright red, as if the hand that he had pressed against his mouth was keeping all his breath in and he might explode at any moment.

"Oh, yes," she said softly. She turned back to the board and wrote "$\frac{4}{9}$" after the times sign. She studied it for a minute and then wrote "$= \frac{12}{36}$" as the answer. She looked to Mr. Ryan for approval. "Is that right?" she asked uncertainly.

"You forgot to reduce," he said.

At that, B.G. and Sheila burst out into a fit of giggles, which started an epidemic of snickers and smothered hoots. Fat, pink, blushing Ruth just stood there, probably wishing that she had made any other mistake on that problem but forgetting to reduce.

"Quiet!" shouted Mr. Ryan. He slapped a book down on his desk. He got almost instant silence. He usually did.

"Now you can reduce after you multiply and come out with the right answer, but the best way to do it is to reduce to the lowest common denominator first, before you do the multiplying. That makes it much easier."

He went over to Ruth and took the chalk from her hand and showed her how to do the problem on the board, crossing out the 4's and the 3 and the 9. Only Ruth wasn't watching the numerals he was writing on the board. She was gazing up at his face, unable to take her eyes off it for a minute. Her mouth hung slightly open. She looked more like a devoted puppy than ever.

"Do you understand?" he asked finally.

She nodded, still gazing at him.

Mr. Ryan began to look really uncomfortable.

"All right, go sit down."

She glided back to her seat with the same dazed stare she'd come into the room with. Stuffy had his head down on his desk, cradled in his arms.

Mr. Ryan, still looking a little flustered himself, spotted Stuffy's odd position. "Aren't you feeling well, Stafford?" he snapped. "Or maybe you don't get enough sleep?"

Stuffy raised his head. "Fine," he said weakly. "Fine."

"Then maybe you'll do the next example for us."

Stuffy limped to the chalkboard and did $\frac{2}{3} \times \frac{5}{8}$ in about six seconds. He didn't even wait for Mr. Ryan to tell him he got it right.

"Well," Mr. Ryan said grumpily, "glad you're awake."

By three o'clock I was as bored with Ruth's "romance" as I'd been with her scrapbooks. Most of the time I had to rely on Stuffy's reactions to Ruth's reactions, since I couldn't see her face when she was at her desk. The secret smiles I had pictured us exchanging were not nearly as much fun as I'd thought they'd be, because only Stuffy was smiling. I had no smiles to exchange. After all, I couldn't see anything to smile at.

Stuffy, on the other hand, was so exhausted from all that held-in laughter, that he claimed he could hardly walk home.

"Hold me up, Wallis." he begged, pretending to stagger out of the schoolyard onto the street. "I'll never make it."

Ding Dong was staying for extra help with fractions, so we didn't have to worry about anyone asking questions.

"I thought I'd croak, I really did," he said. "I don't know how you kept from cracking up."

"Oh, well," I said vaguely. He was enjoying himself so much that I didn't want to tell him it hadn't been hard at all to keep from cracking up.

"How about that dress?" I added, trying to get into the spirit of the thing. "Wasn't that incredible?"

"Yeah. She looked even worse than usual. I wonder what she'll wear tomorrow."

"Maybe a bridal gown," I said weakly. My heart wasn't in it.

"Yeah. Just in case." Stuffy cackled.

"Hey, listen, Stuffy," I said, suddenly remembering what I'd been meaning to ask him since yesterday. "How come you didn't want me to tell Ding Dong anything about my house?"

I had eaten lunch with Bonnie and Lynn. Lynn had started right in asking about the ghost, and I sort of shrugged and said, "You never know," like Stuffy had with Ding Dong. Then I quickly changed the subject. But I didn't want to go on doing that, with Bonnie anyway. She was really nice and seemed very open and honest. That's the kind of a friend you tell things to, not keep things from, and that was exactly the kind of friend I always wanted.

"Oh, yeah," Stuffy said, smacking his forehead. "That's what I meant to tell you. I had this great idea."

"Another one?" I could see I was going to have trouble keeping track of Stuffy's "great ideas."

"What about the worms?"

"Cut the worms."

"Yecch! Stuffy, that's awful."

"I mean, hold the worms."

"What are you *talking* about?"

"*Forget about the worms* is what I'm talking about," he said impatiently.

"Aww, and after you've worked so hard with them. I thought up good names too, if you wanted to have them mating instead of wrestling. Ricardo and Lola."

"That's beautiful," he said. "I'll make a note of that." He stopped in the street and actually jotted the names down in his assignment book. He stuck the book back in his pants pocket. "But Madison Square Garden'll have to wait. First, we're going to find the ghost in your house."

"What ghost? Stuffy, I really don't think—"

"The ghost of Mr. Tucker that's going to haunt your house until his spirit finds rest."

"You really think he's there?" I asked. "I mean, the first night I knew about him I thought—"

"We're going to find out," Stuffy said firmly. "Once and for all. Then poor Mr. Tucker and your whole, terrified family can live in peace once more."

"Well, we're not exactly—"

"Who knows what the ghost will do if he keeps on being frustrated?" Stuffy demanded. "He may be on his good behavior now, thinking you're going to help him, but as time goes by and he realizes no one cares . . ." He let the threatening sentence trail off, leaving my imagination to finish it.

"Uh, what exactly is it that we're going to do to help this—well, whatever you think he is?"

"We're going to hold a séance. In the very room where Mr. Tucker got his brains blown out."

ELEVEN

At first I didn't like the idea of the séance at all.

Number one, Stuffy seemed so convinced that the ghost of Mr. Tucker was hanging around my house just *waiting* that I got nervous all over again and slept with the light on two nights in a row.

Number two, if he *was* hanging around the house, but being nice and quiet and not bothering anyone, why stir things up with a séance and *try* to make him communicate with us? I didn't have anything to say to the ghost of Mr. Tucker, and I sincerely hoped he didn't have anything he wanted to say to me.

Number three, if he wasn't there, the séance, designed to contact Those on the Other Side, might just attract him to the house, like sending an engraved invitation. Who needed *that?*

But Stuffy was smart. I mean, he wasn't only smart about thinking up neat ideas and multiplying fractions and things like that. He was smart about people, too. For instance, he reminded me that Sheila, Teddy, and B.G. were really interested in me now that they knew my house might be haunted. And since I was too shy, he told me, to just ask them over for a visit, holding a séance might be a good excuse to invite them. Along with a lot of other girls. It would be almost like a party. I would make *friends*.

"And I'll handle everything," Stuffy promised. "You won't have to worry about a thing. And we'll hold it on Hallowe'en, so it'll be almost like a Hallowe'en party. All you have to do is get your parents to let us hold the séance in their bedroom. You might not want to tell them it's a séance, though," he added.

"Well what am I supposed to tell them we *do* want to do in their bedroom?" I asked sarcastically.

Stuffy scowled. "Better tell them it's a séance," he admitted. "They'll probably just laugh at the idea anyway."

Actually, if I told my parents the whole scheme, they'd probably contribute black candles, a crystal ball, and a case of soda, and be absolutely delighted that a big bunch of kids was coming to the house for the evening. So I knew that would be no problem.

And that was the right approach. Just think of it like a party. It would be the first party I had ever given, and the more I thought about it, the more excited I got. After all, wouldn't Teddy and Sheila and B.G. and Bonnie all ask me to their parties if I asked them to mine? Stuffy might call it a séance, but they were coming to my house on Hallowe'en, and we would have refreshments, so wasn't that a party? And when you invited people to your house, they had to invite you back to theirs. That was only polite.

Of course, I hadn't invited Ruth to my house.

But that was different. That was *Ruth*.

Another plus was that the more Stuffy thought about the séance, and planned for it, the less he thought about Ruth and Mr. Ryan. By Friday, when Ruth hadn't done anything more outrageous than blush a lot and giggle less than usual, I figured Stuffy had gotten bored with the whole idea and would now "cut the letters" just like he had "cut the worms."

So I finally agreed to hold the séance on Hallowe'en.

"Great!" said Stuffy. "Just leave everything to me."

I told my parents that night. Just as I thought, they laughed at the idea of the séance, but were thrilled with the prospect of my throwing a party. Right away my mother got a piece of paper from the kitchen drawer and started making lists. People to invite, stuff to buy, decorations, etc.

My father said he could get a skeleton from one of those grungy souvenir stores he'd been shopping in. (He'd gotten a glass ball with water in it that snowed over the New York City skyline; a giant pen in the shape of the Empire State building that wrote in twelve different colors, but was so fat it was hard to hold; and a planter formed like a New York Jets football helmet to add to my collection.)

"This is a great skeleton," he said enthusiastically. "It's only plastic, but it's phosphorescent. It glows in the dark. It'll have a terrific effect."

"Does it have 'I LOVE NEW YORK' printed on its ribs?" I asked.

"No," he said, pulling my hair affectionately.

"Then what's the point?" I giggled.

So what difference did it make if I slept with the light on for a few days, just until I got over my fresh attack of nerves? *"Wallis sleeps with a night-light."* A little fear was a small price to pay for the friends I would make and all the invitations I'd be getting after Hallowe'en.

And Stuffy would be so busy planning the séance, he'd forget all about Ruth.

Or so I thought.

Sunday morning my father brought in the papers and said, "Stafford W. Sternwood requests your presence on the front steps."

"Stuffy? So early? Must be about the séance. How did you know his name was Stafford W.?"

"He told me. He actually said, 'Would you please tell Wallis that Stafford W. Sternwood would like to see her.'"

"Sounds like a very nice boy," my mother said approvingly.

"Sounds like something out of the eighteenth century," my father muttered.

I hurried outside.

"Hi, Stuffy. What's up?" I sat down next to him on the steps. He had a pad and pencil in his hand.

"It's time," he said, "to stir things up a little. We're going to write another letter to Ruth."

"What?"

"Another letter to Ruth," he repeated. "It's been a whole week. It's time."

"Time for what? Why? We did that already. Why do another one?"

"To see what happens next."

"What could happen? It'll be the same thing all over again." And, I didn't add out loud, it wasn't that great the first time around.

"Not necessarily," he said, narrowing his eyes to a leer. "It depends on what we write."

"Oh, Stuffy, don't you have enough to do, what with the séance, and the worms, and—"

"Cut the worms," he reminded me.

"Oh, yeah, I forgot. Cut the worms."

"Don't worry about me," Stuffy said. "I've got everything under control."

"Famous last words," I grumbled.

"Come on, Wallis, you know I can't do it without you. I *need* you. You have a talent for that gloppy stuff. And we really need another letter. Nothing's been happening for two days now."

"But Stuffy, I thought we were only going to do that one letter. I mean, you didn't tell me you'd want more. I put all my best stuff into that one. I don't think I can write anything else that good."

"Don't be silly. A talent like yours doesn't just disappear. Now come on, Wallis. I need you."

You have to be a friend to make a friend. Stuffy needed me. And he was the first friend I'd made here. In fact, so far he was the *only* friend I'd made here.

"I'm helping you with the séance, aren't I?" he added.

I looked up at him. If I didn't help him with the letter, was he threatening not to help me with the séance? But it was Stuffy who wanted to have the séance in the first place. It was his idea.

Of course, now that he knew how eager I was to have all those kids come to my house, he sort of had something to persuade me with. But Stuffy wouldn't *blackmail* me into helping him with the letter. Would he?

I studied his face. The blue eyes behind the glasses were innocent. He didn't look mean or threatening. He just looked like Stuffy, asking for help.

Whether he was blackmailing me or begging me, I knew I was going to have to do it. Because I *had* to have that séance. It was going to be the very thing I needed to get me in with Sheila, Teddy, and B.G. And Bonnie, too. Bonnie had been friendly enough at lunch, but she hadn't asked me to her house or anything, and I didn't expect Sheila or the others to. But after the séance . . . things might really begin to work out for me at last, and I wouldn't just have one friend, but maybe more friends than I'd ever had in my life.

But no Stuffy, no séance. Because I didn't know the first thing about contacting Spirits.

"All right," I sighed, "I'll do it."

"Great, Wallis. And this'll be even better than the last. You'll see. This'll be a *killer*."

Dearest, darling Ruth,
I promised myself I would not write to you again, but my hart wouldn8t listen to what my head was telling it. I know that it can never be, that it is madness, sheer madness to even risk putting into words the extasy that I feel when I gaze on you every day. You are the sun and the moon, the morning and the evening star, my day begins and ends with you. Though our love can never

---

blosson, but must whither on the vine like
dying fruit, there is one thing you can do
for me to let me know that my most secret
inmost feelings are shared by you. if you
care for me even a little, send me a secret
message. Do not say ∦ anything or write to
me. that would be xx Too dangerous. Just do
this. wear purple on Thrusday. Then i will
know. Maybe somewhere, somehow, in a different world, in a better life, things
would have worked out for us. But since I
cannot have you, I must learn to live with
this unending pain.
Make a heartsck man feel just one moment of
joy. Wear purple on Thrusday. I will be
waiting. I will not rest till I know your
answexr.
Your beloved till the End of Time.
                              James Ryan.

I sat back from the typewriter and wriggled my stiff
fingers.

"Ah, gee, Stuffy, I don't know. . . ."

"What's the matter with you? It's fantastic."

Really, most of it was Stuffy's ideas. I just sort of said
what he wanted the letter to say a little classier than he
could write it.

"Yeah, I know."

"It's a killer, isn't it?"

"Oh, it's a killer all right."

"Then what's wrong? You're not starting to *like* Ruth
or anything?"

———————

"No! I can't *stand* Ruth. I mean, who could like Ruth the Doof?"

"So? It'll be a riot seeing what she digs up to wear on Thursday."

"Yeah. I guess."

"You're probably just tired from all that typing," Stuffy decided. "You need a rest. I know what. You make a list of all the people you want to ask to the séance, so I'll know how many to plan for."

"How many should I ask?"

"How big is your parents' bedroom?"

"Oh, gee, I don't know. Pretty big, I guess. Not huge."

"Well, as many as you think can fit. The more the merrier."

"You think a big séance is a good idea?"

Stuffy beamed with pleasure. "I think a big séance is a *great* idea."

When I got home, Grandma was sitting in the kitchen, drinking a cup of coffee with my mother and father.

"Grandma! What a surprise!" I ran to hug and kiss her. "Why didn't you tell me Grandma was coming?"

My mother smiled weakly. "We didn't know, dear. It was a surprise to us, too."

"I just got up this morning and thought, it was so nice talking to Wallis on the phone the other day, I just *have* to see her. So I hopped on the train and here I am. I brought some cake and cookies too. Over there on the counter." She pointed. "Go take something."

I ripped open the white bakery boxes.

"Wallis, you haven't had lunch yet," my mother said. "You'll spoil your appetite."

"No I won't." I stuffed a tiny, chocolate-sprinkled butter cookie into my mouth and reached for another one.

"Wallis!"

"Oh, let her eat, Lainie. She's a growing girl."

"Did you hear about my séa—my party, Grandma?" I asked, through a mouthful of crumbs.

"Don't talk with your mouth full," Grandma said automatically. "What party?"

"Wallis is holding a séance," my father said, grinning. "On Hallowe'en. They're going to try to communicate with Mr. Tucker's ghost."

Grandma frowned. "Do you think that's a good idea, Jerry? There are some things man was not meant to tamper with, you know."

"Oh, Ma, you've been watching those horror movies again!" he laughed.

Grandma shrugged. "So? Some people drink. I watch horror movies. Just because something is in a movie doesn't mean it isn't true."

"It's just a party, Mother. You know, the kids getting into the Hallowe'en spirit." My mother jumped up and snatched the cookie box out of my hands.

"I'm not sure kids should be getting into spirits at all," Grandma said.

"That's cute, Ma," my father said, trying hard to sound jolly. "Getting into spirits? Like liquor? Get it?"

"I didn't mean it to be cute. I'm not being cute. There are more things on heaven and earth, Horatio, than you ever dreamed of. And that's not from movies, Jerry. That's *Shakespeare*. I think Shakespeare knew what he was talking about, don't you?"

"Well, it's not going to be a real séance, Grandma. I

mean, it's just for fun. Stuffy is planning the whole thing."

"Well you may think it's just for fun, but They"—she gestured toward the ceiling—"might take you seriously."

"But Grandma, you said you don't believe in ghosts."

"I don't believe in child abuse either, but that doesn't mean it doesn't exist."

Her logic confused me—but I guess my parents couldn't figure it out either. My father scratched his head and my mother looked a little dazed.

"I don't follow you, Ma," my father said.

"All I'm saying is, you don't fool around with what you don't know about. You wouldn't call a plumber to fix your electricity, would you?"

My mother spoke very slowly. "Then you think the children should call in an expert to run the séance?"

Grandma shook her head angrily. "No! I'm saying the children shouldn't hold a séance at all."

"Oh, Grandma," I sighed, "we've got it all planned. We're having it right in the bedroom and everything—"

"*The* bedroom?"

"*The* bedroom," my father nodded.

Grandma sighed deeply and rose to her full five feet nine inches.

"If you don't mind," she said very formally, "I think I'll go into the living room and read the Sunday papers. I didn't have a chance to this morning."

My parents looked over my head at each other. My father shrugged and looked helpless. My mother poured another cup of coffee, and gulped it down like a drunk who's been off the sauce for weeks.

"You want me to tell her we won't have a séance?" I asked.

"You mean, lie?" said my mother.

"Well . . . I'm going to have the séance, no matter what. But if you want me to, I'll tell her I won't. It'll make her feel better."

"I don't want you to lie, Wallis," my mother said.

"You don't think" my father said hopefully, "a *white* lie, to make somebody feel better—"

"No. A lie is a lie. And besides, the truth always comes out in the end. Wallis or you or I will forget and let it slip out, and then she'll know we lied."

"All right, look, I'll tell her I'll think about what she said. How's that?"

"That's good," my mother agreed. "Because you will think about it, that's for sure."

"Oh, I'll *think* about it," I promised.

I went in to sit down on the couch next to Grandma. "Listen, Grandma, about what you said. About the séance? I'll give it a lot of thought, okay?"

She looked up from the News of the Week in Review section and peered at me. "You'll give it a lot of thought? What does that mean?"

"That means I'll think about what you said. About the things man wasn't meant to tamper with."

"And then you'll go and do what you please after you think about it, right?"

I looked down at the floor. Even though I didn't see Grandma more than a few times a year, I knew her well enough. I should have remembered that she was not the kind of person you could put off with an "I'll think about it."

"I'll make up my own mind, yes, Grandma. After I think about what you said."

She shook her head, but there was a little smile on her lips, as if she couldn't help it, even if she really didn't feel like smiling. She grabbed me by the shoulders and squeezed. Hard. (Grandma really doesn't know her own strength.)

"You're my granddaughter, all right. There's no doubt about that."

"I think that's fine, Grandma. Don't you?"

She grinned. I rubbed my shoulder.

T W E L V E

Among Stuffy's other talents, it turned out he was artistic.

On Monday morning he showed me a sample invitation he'd drawn. There was a crystal ball on the front, with sparks coming out of it. Over it was printed "YOUR PRESENCE IS REQUESTED" and under it "AT A SEANCE."

Inside he'd written my name and address, and Oct. 31, 7:30 P.M. Then, under that: "HELP US COMMUNICATE WITH A TORTURED SOUL ON THE OTHER SIDE."

"Gee, Stuffy, that's beautiful," I said admiringly. "But couldn't we put 'party' instead of 'séance'?"

"Nah. Everyone gives parties. But if they know they might meet the ghost of Mr. Tucker, they'll come in droves. He's what you call our drawing card. Now do you have a list of people you want to invite?"

"Yeah. I made it up last night. It's pretty short, though."

I gave it to him. The only names on it were Sheila, Teddy, B. G., Bonnie, and Lynn.

"Five people? It's hardly worth it for only five people."

"Well, those are the only people I know. I couldn't think of anyone else. Except Ruth—and I don't want her."

"How about Ding Dong and Packy? You know them."

"I hardly know Packy at all. And Ding Dong . . . well . . ."

"Look, why don't you let me make up a list of who to invite? I know more people than you do, and I'll just invite nice ones. It wouldn't even be much of a party with only five people."

"But I won't know some of them," I said.

"Yeah, but I'll be there to help you. And you'll know them afterwards. Trust me, Wallis. After this, you'll have loads of friends."

"Well, okay."

"I'll make up all the invitations and mail them out."

"You better put my phone number on them," I suggested, "so we'll know who's coming. We have to know how much food to get."

Stuffy frowned. "I wouldn't bother with having people call you," he said casually. "After all, you won't even know some of them and that might be sort of embarrassing. Just plan for about fifteen."

I didn't even think to wonder why it would be embarrassing for people I didn't know to call me when I heard how many people Stuffy planned to invite. All the séances I'd ever seen in the movies or on TV had just a few people gathered around a table, holding hands. Certainly no more than six. We didn't have a table in the house that would seat fifteen people, and even if we did, we probably couldn't fit it in the bedroom.

"Fifteen sounds like a lot," I said doubtfully.

"They might not all come," Stuffy pointed out. "But we have to plan for that many, just in case."

"Oh. Okay. But look, I don't think it's fair for you to do all those invitations yourself. Why don't I come over to your house tonight and help out? You're doing too much."

"No, no," said Stuffy hastily. "I like to do them. And I'm good at it too. Just leave everything to me."

By Thursday, when no one had said a word to me about coming to the séance, I began to worry that maybe I shouldn't have left everything to Stuffy.

Early Thursday morning I met him on the way to school. All he could talk about was whether Ruth would wear purple today, as our letter had asked. All I wanted to talk about was why no one was talking to me about my party.

"Wallis, I told you to leave everything to me, didn't I?"

"But Hallowe'en is Sunday, Stuffy. Didn't you mail the invitations out, or what?"

"Of course I did. Stop worrying. You know how slow the mail is."

"But if you mailed them out Monday night—"

"I couldn't get them all done Monday night. Some I mailed out Tuesday night. And if the mail isn't delivered until the kids are in school, they wouldn't get them until this afternoon. I wonder what Ruth is going to find that's purple to wear!"

"Maybe she won't wear purple," I said hopefully. "Maybe she doesn't care about Mr. Ryan anymore."

"Are you kidding?" shrieked Stuffy. "You saw her yesterday. She was practically wiped out after that second letter."

"Yeah," I said dully. Actually, I hadn't seen that much of her because like last week, it was Stuffy who had the best view of how Ruth was acting once she took her seat. But what I had seen—when she walked into class, her eyes fixed on the floor, and how she stuttered and mumbled and missed the easiest questions that Mr. Ryan asked—was enough to convince me that it wasn't a bit funny watching someone being "wiped out." Not even Ruth the Doof.

I began to feel sorrier and sorrier for her, which made me angry, because I didn't want to feel sorry for her. I didn't like her, and I wasn't ever going to like her, and if I hadn't gotten involved in this stupid joke, I wouldn't *have* to feel sorry for her.

I promised myself that as soon as the séance was over, I was going to have nothing more to do with Stuffy's letters to Ruth, if he had any plans to send more. By then, I would have plenty of friends, and I wouldn't have to depend on Stuffy's company alone. If he wanted to stop being my friend because I wouldn't help him with the letters, well then, he wasn't that good a friend to begin with.

We were the first ones in class again. Mr. Ryan was writing on the chalkboard when we came in.

"Good morning, Mr. Ryan," we chorused. What

good little students we sounded like, I thought. If only he knew!

"Good morning. You certainly are the early birds today. Maybe one of you would open a few windows? It's pretty warm in here."

"I'll do it," Stuffy volunteered. It *was* warm in there. Stuffy got the window pole and opened all the windows from the top.

"They seem to have the thermostat up to eighty again," Mr. Ryan remarked.

"You don't even need any heat today," Stuffy said. He put the window pole back in its rack. "It's really warm out."

"Just wait till the middle of January," Mr. Ryan warned. "That's when they'll turn the heat off entirely."

Stuffy slid into the seat next to me. "The school buses are in," he whispered. "I saw them out the window. It's a good thing we got here in time. I think they're early." He could hardly sit still. "This was a brilliant idea," he added. "The purple, I mean."

"Brilliant," I muttered.

"Isn't the suspense *killing* you?" he hissed. "You know, will she, won't she?"

"Yeah, killing me."

He twisted in the seat and looked at me searchingly. "Hey, Wallis, what's the matter with—"

He stopped abruptly and stared at the door. He clutched my wrist so hard I thought it would break. I turned. There was Ruth, framed in the doorway, pausing a moment as if she was a beautiful actress making an entrance at a fancy party.

She was wearing the only thing I had ever seen her wear that was too big on her. It was a bright purple bulky knit sweater with little dots of white scattered over it like seeds, and a blue skirt. The sweater was enormous, with a heavy cowl collar that drooped halfway down her chest, and sleeves that nearly reached her fingertips. She was already perspiring, her frizzy hair sticking damply to her forehead. She was dressed just right for the North Pole.

"She must have gone out and bought that special," Stuffy whispered. "That was probably the only thing she could find in purple."

A bunch of kids had piled up behind Ruth, and now pushed her impatiently into the room as they bustled in. She stumbled, caught her dangling sleeve on the doorknob, and dropped two books, right at Mr. Ryan's feet.

Mr. Ryan looked around, as if trying to find out who'd pushed her. Nobody offered to help Ruth pick up her books, and for a moment she just stood there, staring at Mr. Ryan.

"If she says, 'See, I'm wearing purple,' I'll croak," Stuffy threatened.

"If she does, we may both croak," I said. It suddenly occurred to me that if Ruth ever actually said anything to Mr. Ryan, Stuffy and I could be in Very Big Trouble. Hot as it was, I shivered.

They both bent down at the same time and practically bumped heads picking up Ruth's books. Ruth gave him such a smile of gratitude that you would have thought he was rescuing her from pirates.

"How can she stand that sweater today?" I murmured. "It looks so heavy."

I prayed that she wouldn't say anything to Mr. Ryan.

She said something, but with the din around us, I couldn't hear what it was. Probably just thank you, though, because Mr. Ryan simply nodded and turned back to the chalkboard. Ruth walked to her seat looking very disappointed.

"She must have expected him to propose on the spot," Stuffy tittered.

"You better just hope *she* doesn't propose to *him*," I warned.

Arthur Deegan was standing patiently next to his desk, as usual, saying nothing, just waiting for Stuffy to get up. Stuffy hauled himself out of the seat, nodded weakly to Arthur, and went to sit at his own desk.

"He your boyfriend?" Arthur mumbled. He was busily shoving books into his desk and didn't even look at me as he spoke. I couldn't believe I heard him right. It was maybe the third time Arthur had spoken to me since we'd been sitting next to each other, and the first two times he'd asked to borrow a pen.

Had he really said that?

He didn't repeat it, but he looked up at me as if he was expecting an answer.

"Of course not!" I said. "He's a friend, and he's a boy. That doesn't make him my *boyfriend*."

"Oh," Arthur said.

"Besides, what difference does it make to you?"

Arthur shrugged. "No difference. I don't care."

"Then why did you ask?" I persisted.

He shrugged again. "Just wondering."

Weird, I thought. Four weeks and hardly a word, and now this. Did Arthur *like* me? I didn't think Arthur liked anyone.

"I always see you walking home with him," he added.

Before I could stop myself I snapped, "What are you,

---

a private detective or something? Are you *watching* me?" *Don't be so prickly, Wallis,* I could hear my mother saying. Well, I couldn't help it. Quiet, mysterious Arthur Deegan was making me very nervous with all this sudden interest in my boyfriends.

"Not watching," he said mildly. "Just seeing. I can't help seeing you, can I?"

I buried my head in a book, hoping Arthur wouldn't notice my confusion. For the rest of the morning, I didn't even think to look and see how Ruth was holding up. I just kept shifting my eyes sideways to sneak a look at Arthur Deegan every time I had a chance.

Maybe he did like me. Why else would he have wanted to know if Stuffy was my boyfriend? Once I peeked over at Arthur and found he was staring at me. I nearly jumped in my seat. I fixed my eyes on the math test on my desk, but I was too rattled to concentrate. The fractions swam in front of me; they made no sense. It was like trying to read a foreign language in an alphabet you've never seen before.

What in the world had come over Arthur Deegan?

Three o'clock and still no one had mentioned the séance to me. I didn't want to bring it up myself, because what if they'd all decided they didn't want to come? If Stuffy had sent out some of the invitations Monday night, at least some kids should have gotten them by now. Why wasn't anyone talking to me about it? The party was only four days away.

I waited for Stuffy to collect his books and then followed him out the door and down the steps. I wondered if Arthur Deegan was watching me, but I didn't want to look around, in case he was.

"Hey, Stuffy, nobody's said a word to me about the séance yet. Are you sure you sent out those invitations?"

Eddie Bell, clumping along beside us, said, "What séance?"

"Well, to tell you the truth, Wallis, I didn't finish them all as fast as I thought I would. But everybody will definitely have them by tomorrow."

"Am I invited?" asked Ding Dong. "What's a séance?"

"Stuffy, you promised! What if everybody has something else to do that night? What if someone else is giving a party? Why did you wait so long? Why didn't you let me help you?"

"Are you serious?" Stuffy asked Ding Dong. "You don't know what a séance is?"

"No," said Eddie, sounding surly. "I don't know what a séance is. Do *you?*"

"I'm *giving* it, Ding Dong," Stuffy retorted. "Don't you think I know what it is I'm giving?"

"*I'm* giving it," I said angrily. "It's at my house. If anyone comes," I added.

"Well, I'm running it, then," Stuffy said. "And they'll come. Everyone will come. You'll see. Trust me, Wallis. Have I ever let you down before?"

"I've only known you a couple of weeks!" I shouted.

"At your house?" asked Ding Dong. "Am I invited?"

Suddenly I felt very stupid. I didn't know *anything* about this séance I was having in four days. Not even who my guests were going to be.

"I don't know," I muttered. "Stuffy handled all that.

Just who *is* invited, Stuffy? I mean, I'd like to know who I'm inviting to my own party."

"All the kids you wanted, plus some others I thought would be good."

"Who? What others?" He reeled off the rest of the names. Arthur Deegan was included. So were Eddie and Packy.

"Does that mean I'm coming?" Eddie asked. "And is it a party or a séance?"

"Sure you can come," said Stuffy generously. I glared at him. I never would have invited Ding Dong to my party. Or Packy either.

"And it's a combination," Stuffy went on. "Party and séance. For the séance part we're going to get in touch with the ghost of Mr. Tucker. You know, the guy that's haunting Wallis' house."

"Oh yeah?" said Eddie. "You gonna have stuff to eat?"

"Sure," I said.

"Eddie, don't you hear what I'm telling you? We're going to be communicating with a *ghost*. Did you ever talk to a ghost before? This could be the experience of a *lifetime*."

"Yeah? Well I once met Julius Erving," said Eddie.

Stuffy shook his head hopelessly. Eddie was driving him crazy. Ding Dong was a pain, but with him around, Stuffy couldn't cackle over Ruth and her purple sweater and her imaginary romance. I was so angry at Stuffy by now, and so worried that this great party I'd been looking forward to would never come off, that if he'd said one word about Ruth to me, I might have blown our whole love letter conspiracy right there.

_____

I mean, who cared about Ruth now?

What with everything else I had on my mind, including the new mystery of Arthur Deegan, the only thing I'd noticed Ruth do all day was sweat.

Watching Ruth sweat was not my idea of big yoks.

THIRTEEN

When my father called me to the phone that night I thought that someone was finally calling about the séance. I snatched the receiver from his hand.

"Hello?"

"Wallis?"

Ruth. Annoyed and disappointed, I didn't even try to hide my feelings. "What do you want?"

"Wallis, I have to talk to you. Can you come over to my house?"

"*Now?*"

"Tomorrow. After school. You could come home on the bus with me."

Oh, sure, and have Sheila and Teddy and B.G. see me getting chummy with her again.

"No, I can't. I'm busy tomorrow."

"What about Saturday morning, then?"

Saturday my mother and I were going shopping to get stuff for the party. "No. I'm busy Saturday too."

"Sunday?" asked Ruth desperately. "What about Sunday?"

The day of the séance. To which Ruth wasn't invited.

"No, Sunday I'm going to be *very* busy. Look, I'm busy this whole weekend." My father frowned at me. I turned my back so I wouldn't see him.

"Wallis, I have a *problem*. I have to talk to somebody."

Why me? I wondered irritably. "Well, look, Ruth, what is it?"

"I can't—I mean, it's not something I can tell you over the phone." Her voice was a bare whisper. I could hardly hear her.

Oh boy. I knew exactly what the problem was. Ruth wanted to talk to me about Mr. Ryan's letters.

What a mess! Why had I let Stuffy talk me into this? If Ruth was pestering me, it was my own fault. If we'd never written those letters, she wouldn't have a problem. At least, not *this* problem. And if we hadn't written those letters I could let her go and talk her problems over with her mother or her father—or anyone else but me, without worrying about her.

But now I had to talk to her. I had to make sure that I was the only one she told about the letters, because if she told somebody else—if the letters were ever traced back—I closed my eyes and swallowed hard.

"Wallis? Are you still there?"

"Yeah, yeah, I'm still here. I was just trying to think of a good time to get together." I thought fast. If she could just hold out till Monday, till after the séance; once that was behind me, and I was sure everything was okay, I could really concentrate on solving this stupid tangle.

"How about Monday night?"

"I can't wait until Monday!" Ruth cried. "I have to talk to someone *now*."

"All right, all right," I said hastily. "I'll come over to your house tomorrow night, okay?" That way, in the dark, no one would see me with her. And maybe it would be best to get the whole thing settled as soon as possible. At least then I wouldn't have to worry that Ruth would crack and spill the story to her mother, or even to Mr. Ryan. Sure, the sooner the better.

I didn't have the slightest idea how I was going to help her settle it, but I knew I'd better come up with something.

"Okay," Ruth sniffled. "Right after dinner?"

"Sure. About seven-thirty."

Friday at lunch, when no one had yet told me they would come to my party, I felt desperate. Sitting with Bonnie and Lynn, I worked up my courage and when the lunch period was practically over, I finally managed to bring up the subject. Even if they told me, no, they didn't want to come, that would be better than not knowing. I mean, there was no point in my parents' spending all that money for food and soda and stuff if no one was going to show up.

"Hey," I said, trying to sound casual, "you guys coming to my party?"

"I thought it was a séance," Lynn said.

At least they'd *heard* about it. "Well, yeah, it's both, actually."

"Sure we're coming," Bonnie said. "I just got the—

invitation yesterday afternoon." Her voice sounded a little strained and I wondered why she hesitated over the word *invitation*.

"It should be worth it," Lynn agreed. The bell rang just then and I wasn't sure I had heard her right. Worth it? What did that mean? Worth what? I wanted to ask her, but she'd already left the table and was dumping her lunch tray.

Oh, well, at least I knew the invitations had gotten sent and that *someone* was coming. I didn't want to push any further, because I didn't want to sound too anxious. I would just assume, like Stuffy had told me, that everyone would come. I didn't know why no one was talking to me about it, but maybe all the invitations had come late, or maybe they just didn't want to say anything in front of someone who hadn't been invited.

That sounded reasonable. I felt much better about the whole thing until I got back to the classroom and sat down next to Arthur Deegan. *He* could have said something to me about it, I realized, without anyone else hearing. Why hadn't *he* mentioned it?

Maybe he thinks *I* like *him!* Maybe he thinks that's why I invited him! Maybe that's why he asked all those questions about whether Stuffy was my boyfriend! The thought was so embarrassing that I spent the whole afternoon with my head buried in my books, not looking at Arthur once. Although I must have looked very studious, I didn't learn much. I spent most of the time wishing—séance or no séance—that I had never heard of anyone named Stafford W. Sternwood.

"Read this," Ruth said. She handed me the first letter we had written. I read it over, as if I had never seen it before, though I practically knew it by heart. When I was finished, I looked up and tried to think of something to say.

"Wow," I managed weakly. "How about that?"

"There's more," she said. She handed me the second letter.

I read that one over too.

"I wore purple on Thursday, like he asked," Ruth said, "and he didn't say one word to me."

"But what did you expect him to say? I mean, he told you you could never talk about it."

"Then what's the point?" Ruth asked. "Why did he write the letters?"

Good question. What *was* the point? I couldn't seem to remember anymore.

"Well, uh, like he said, maybe he just wanted to let you know how he felt."

"*Why?* What good does that do?"

"I don't know," I muttered.

Ruth took the letters from me and stuck them in one of the scrapbooks piled in her closet. She turned around and I could see that she was on the verge of bursting into tears.

"Maybe," I said quickly, without even thinking of what I was going to say, "maybe he just wanted you to know you were loved."

Ruth's face looked like it was going to crumble. She sat down on the floor and put her head in her hands. Her shoulders began to shake.

I never felt worse in my life. Not even when it was *me* doing the crying.

"Ruth—I—"

She wiped her eyes on her sleeve. "Why should he

love me, Wallis?" She stared up at me, her face blotchy and tear-stained. "Why should he? How *can* he? Nobody else does."

"Maybe . . . maybe he—" I struggled for something to say, something that would sound believable. "Maybe he sees something in you that other people don't see yet," I said in a rush.

Ruth's mouth fell open. She didn't say anything, she just sat there, twining her fingers together and sniffling every once in awhile.

Finally she seemed to calm down a little and she said, in a tiny voice, "What should I do?"

I had to stop myself from heaving a loud sigh of relief. I must have said the right things, even though I wasn't sure why they were right. Ruth seemed quiet now, and I was pretty sure she believed what I had told her. She probably wanted to believe it, anyway. I thought, if I were Ruth I'd want to believe it.

"Don't do anything," I said softly. I prayed she would listen to me. "There's nothing you *can* do. If you love him—" she lowered her eyes to the floor "—forget him."

"But Wallis," she cried, "he ought to *know* I love him. He's *suffering*. He said so."

"You wore purple on Thursday, didn't you? So he knows. Ruth, if you love somebody, you don't want to get them in trouble. He'll be in big trouble if anyone ever finds out about this. He'll lose his job. A teacher can't fool around with a student."

"We didn't fool around!" Ruth said indignantly.

"Well, a teacher can't even *say* those things to a student. He can't even *think* them. It's against the law. You're too young. You're a—a—*minor*."

"I want to write him a letter," Ruth said.

"Aren't you listening to one word I'm saying?" I yelled.

"Shh!" hissed Ruth.

"Ruth," I whispered, "you can't. He told you not to."

"Just one letter," she insisted. "Then I'll never talk about it again. Ever. To anyone."

I thought fast. If Ruth meant that—if she kept her promise—maybe that would be the best way to end the whole thing. Ruth would feel better, and I could relax and not worry every day that she'd go running to Mr. Ryan and let everything out. There was only one hitch.

I'd have to make sure that the letter was never mailed.

"All right," I said, still sounding like I didn't approve of what she was doing. "Maybe one last letter wouldn't hurt. And I can mail it for you on my way home."

"I thought I'd just stick it in his mailbox at school," Ruth said.

"Are you *crazy*? What if somebody sees you? Ruth, he'll never forgive you if he gets fired on account of you. How could you do that to someone you love?"

"All right, Wallis," she said tiredly. "I'll mail it. Would you help me write it? I'm not very good at writing, and I've never had to write a love letter before."

Oh, this was so *weird*. First I help Stuffy write love letters to Ruth, then I help Ruth write love letters *replying* to the love letters I had written. I felt very strange. Like I had a split personality and one of my personalities was madly in love with the other.

But it was the best way to make sure that the fake

romance would finally end, and I jumped at the chance to bring the whole stupid joke to a permanent—and safe—finish.

"Sure. Get some paper."

Ruth opened her top desk drawer and got out a box of stationery. I looked at it as she opened the lid. The paper was lined in red and at the top of the sheet was a picture of Snoopy and Woodstock standing on a mailbox. As she sat down next to me on the floor, I read the little balloon coming out of Snoopy's mouth. It said, "Have a nice day."

Wasn't that just like Ruth, using Snoopy stationery to write a love letter? It was so ridiculous that for a moment I forgot that the letter was never going to be mailed, so it didn't make any difference what kind of stationery she used.

"What should I say?" she asked.

"What do you want to say?"

"I don't know." She bit the end of the pen.

"Well, how about this: 'Even though you said not to write, I couldn't help it. I just want you to know that—'"

Ruth copied down every word, writing very fast. "Hold it, wait," she said, trying to catch up. I sighed. I wondered if my career would turn out to be ghostwriting other people's books. I certainly seemed to be in demand as a letter writer these days.

"Okay. Go ahead."

"—'knowing you love me has made me very happy.'" I paused, waiting for her to finish the sentence. "'I realize that I must never—' underline that," I ordered. She nodded "Twice," I added. Obediently, she drew another line under it. "'Must never speak to you or write to you again, and I promise I never will. Even though we never really had a beginning, this must be the end.'"

Ruth gazed at me, tears beginning to well up again in her pale little eyes. "Oh, Wallis," she breathed, "that's *beautiful.*"

"I seem to have a knack for this," I muttered.

"What?"

"Never mind, never mind. Go on and write. 'I will never forget your love but I give you my solemn oath that no one will ever know of this and that I will never mention it again. *Ever.*'"

She wrote furiously.

"You might want to add, 'till the day I die' but that's up to you. Makes it a little stronger, you know?"

"Oh, Wallis, it's perfect. It's just what I wanted to say."

She signed it "Your beloved till the End of Time," just like he—I mean, *we*—had signed the letters to her. She stuck it in an envelope and addressed it to the school.

"I'll put 'Personal' on it," she said, "so no one else will open it by mistake."

"Good idea."

She wrote "PRIVATE" on it too, just to make sure. If I had been *Mrs.* Ryan and that letter had come for him at home, I would have ripped it open on the spot.

"I'll get a stamp," Ruth said. She lumbered out of the room and I sat there on the floor, holding the letter in my hand. This was really no guarantee that she wasn't, some time, going to talk. Promises could be broken— even solemn oaths. Just because she wrote the letter that I dictated didn't mean she wouldn't change her mind and go panting to Mr. Ryan next week. She said that we'd written exactly what she wanted to say, but I had done all the writing, and when she had a chance to think about it, maybe she would decide that even if Mr. Ryan lost his job, it would be worth living on welfare with the man she loved.

Well, I did the best I could. It was a rotten, crummy, unfunny joke and it was up to me to clean up the mess Stuffy and I had made of Ruth's feelings. If I didn't sleep one night till I was out of that school, it would serve me right. I deserved to feel guilty. I deserved to have sleepless nights. It was my own fault.

By the time Ruth tiptoed back into the room with a stamp, I was almost ready to throw myself at her feet and confess the whole thing, just to stop feeling like such a criminal.

But one look at her beaming face and I thought better of it. Telling Ruth the truth was not going to make *her* feel better, even if it took a load off *my* mind.

"I'm so glad I could talk to you, Wallis," she said. She licked the stamp and stuck it on the letter. "You were a big help. You're the best friend I ever had."

I'm the *only* friend you ever had, I thought grimly. And some friend at that.

"I feel much better." She handed me the letter. "You promise you'll mail that on the way home?" She took it back and held it against her lips for a moment. "Maybe I better mail it myself."

I snatched it out of her hands and stuck it in my jeans pocket before she could change her mind again. "But don't expect an answer, right? It's over, right?"

Ruth sighed. "Yes, I guess so. It was impossible

anyway. I mean, I really knew that all the time. But it was nice while it lasted."

"*Nice?* But Ruth, it made you *miserable.*"

Ruth managed a sickly little grin.

"Yeah, Wallis, but I've been miserable a lot of times, and this was the first time I was miserable because somebody *liked* me."

I looked away, too embarrassed to face her.

When I got home, I tore the letter into a hundred pieces and threw it into my wastepaper basket.

FOURTEEN

Stuffy came over at six Sunday night lugging two large shopping bags. At first my father thought he was another trick-or-treater and tried to drop some candy in one of the bags.

"It's me, Mr. Greene. Stafford W. Sternwood."

"Oh."

"I'm not trick or treating. I came to set up the stuff for the séance."

"I see. Well, come on in. You can have some candy anyway."

"Thanks a lot. No, don't drop that in the bags!" he cried as my father held two candy bars out.

"What's in there anyway?" my father asked. He stuck the candy in Stuffy's coat pocket.

"Oh, just some stuff," Stuffy said mysteriously.

We went upstairs and I flipped the light switch on in

the bedroom. I was beginning to be almost as nervous about the ghost of Mr. Tucker showing up at the séance as I was about the fifteen people Stuffy had invited.

What if Mr. Tucker did materialize? What if he *was* tormented and was just waiting around for a convenient séance to let us know how miserable he was? What if he said, "Wallis, get out of my house"?

Not that I actually believed in ghosts or anything. . . . But there *are* some things man was not meant to tamper with. Right, Grandma.

"Not bad, not bad," Stuffy said, surveying the room. "We can sit on the floor, sort of in a semicircle around the bed. He *was* shot in bed, right?"

"Not in *this* bed."

Stuffy shrugged. "Doesn't matter. A bed's a bed. Now, Wallis, don't you have something to do? Unwrap the potato chips or get dressed or something?"

I looked down at my sweater and skirt. "I *am* dressed," I said. "Isn't this okay?"

"Oh, yeah, that's fine. What I meant was, I have some things I want to take care of in here, so why don't you, uh, take care of things out *there*." He gestured toward the door.

"Are you trying to get rid of me?" I demanded. "What things do you want to do in here?"

Stuffy put the shopping bags down on the floor. He took a deep breath. "Look, Wallis, we want this to be a really *good* séance, right?"

"Right," I said doubtfully. What did he mean, "good"?

"Well then, I have to make sure that it turns out the way we want it to."

"What way is that?"

"Realistic. Scary. With a ghost."

"Wait a minute! Wait a minute! You're going to make *sure* the ghost of Mr. Tucker comes? You're going to *make* this realistic? Just what is it you're going to set up in here?"

"Never mind. It's better if you don't know. That way you'll seem just as scared as everyone else."

"Stuffy, do you mean to tell me you're going to *fake* this séance? I'm giving a fixed séance? With a phony ghost?"

He stared at me. "Well, what did you expect?"

"You mean, you didn't think the real ghost would show up at all?"

"Real ghost?" Stuffy echoed. "Are you kidding, Wallis?"

I just stood there, my mouth hanging open, looking, I suppose, as dumb as I always thought Ruth looked.

"You mean," I said finally, "you don't believe in ghosts? You didn't believe in the ghost of Mr. Tucker all along?"

He looked at me as if he thought I was crazy. "Did *you?*"

I sank down on the bed. How could he do this to me? How did I let myself get involved in this? Why had I ever asked Stafford W. Sternwood the way to Sweetpea Street?

"After all those things you said to Ding Dong," I sputtered, "about Mr. Tucker's tortured soul? And all those things you said to *me?* And the way I let the girls believe—because *you* told me not to tell anyone there was no ghost? And you didn't believe *any* of it?"

"That was just a hype. You know, like a publicity

buildup. Gee, Wallis, I thought you were smart enough to—"

"Ohh!" I groaned. I wanted to tear my hair out. No, I wanted to tear *his* hair out. Someone was sure to suspect that the séance was a fake. And it was *my* séance. The invitations were in *my* name. It was at *my* house. In *my* parents' bedroom. With *my* own, personal ghost. Everyone would think I had been deliberately trying to make fools of them. They'd never forgive me for asking them to a séance and pretending it was real, when all along it was just a trick.

They'd never believe I didn't have anything to do with it. How could they? I had *everything* to do with it. Even if Stuffy had handled all the details, I'd let him handle them. I mean, if I'd wanted to just give a party, I should have worked up the nerve to do my own inviting and run my own party and hoped for the best. But no, I'd let Stuffy go ahead and do anything he wanted to do for this séance, because it was so important to me to have friends—the right friends— that I hadn't even wanted to ask too many questions.

"Look, Wallis, this stuff is like—insurance. And most of it is just for atmosphere anyhow." He reached into one of the bags and pulled out some thick candles and a pair of silver candlesticks. "See? These will make a nice, spooky setting. It's Hallowe'en. You want the right decorations, don't you? I mean, any Hallowe'en party would have decorations, wouldn't it?"

"What's the insurance?" I asked. "Insurance against what?"

"Just in case Mr. Tucker doesn't come when we call him, that's all."

"But you said you don't expect him to!"

"I just meant it's good to be prepared. You want the kids to get their money's worth, don't you?"

"Their money's worth? What do you mean?"

"Nothing, nothing," Stuffy said hastily. "It's just a saying. What I meant was you want them to enjoy themselves. You want them to be glad they came. So just in *case*—"

"I don't want to give a phony séance! They'll think I'm a cheat and a fraud and—"

"They'll be a lot more disappointed if you hold a séance and nothing happens!" Stuffy retorted.

I was getting more confused by the minute.

"Are you or aren't you going to fake this whole thing?" I demanded.

"Not unless I have to," he said. "We'll try it straight first."

"But you don't think it'll work without phonying it up, do you?"

"Who knows," Stuffy said, "what evil lurks in the house of Greene? Look, it's getting late. Do you want to call the whole thing off? Is that what you want? You can still do it. You can get on that phone—" he pointed to the yellow phone on the night table "—and just go un-invite everyone. If you want to ruin everyone's plans, disappoint everyone who's been looking forward to this party for weeks, just go ahead."

"They didn't even get the invitations till a couple of days ago. No one was looking forward to this for weeks."

"Well? Tell me what you want to do, Wallis."

I looked at the clock next to the phone. It was six-thirty. One hour till the party was supposed to begin.

"I'll go unwrap the potato chips," I said.

Was holding a fake séance against the law? I didn't know, but if it was, I was an accomplice again. First, forging letters from a teacher, and now this. Why couldn't Stuffy have just stuck to worm-wrestling?

My mother and I poured cellophane bags of snacks into serving bowls and candy dishes in the kitchen. My mother jabbered away a mile a minute. I couldn't remember ever seeing her so excited.

"This was a good idea," she said. "Just think of all the friends you'll have after tonight. I don't know why we never did it before."

"I never wanted to before. And we never lived in a house where a murder happened before."

"True. Remember when you first heard about the murder? You were furious at us. And now it gives you the perfect excuse to meet people. Isn't it funny how things turn out?"

"Hilarious."

"Hey, how come you're so quiet? I'm more excited about this party than you are."

"I guess I'm a little nervous."

"Of course you are. That's understandable. Where's Stafford?"

"Upstairs. Uh—decorating the bedroom."

"Good idea. Atmosphere is very important for a good party."

That sounded like magazine advice.

"We'll put the food in the dining room, okay? Then after the séance you can come down here and eat and—well, whatever it is you want to do after the séance. You can use the living room too so you should have plenty of space."

"Where will you and Dad be?"

"We'll stay in the den and watch television. I guess you don't want us around."

Oh, boy, was that an understatement. "No. Nobody's parents hang around for a party. You couldn't go to the movies or something?" I asked hopefully.

"No, we couldn't. But we'll stay out of your way, I promise. Anyway, you'll want someone to answer the door for trick-or-treaters. You don't want to be bothered with them in the middle of the séance."

The doorbell rang and she went to answer it. "Speak of the devil," she called back to me.

Nice choice of words.

The hands of the clock dragged towards seven-thirty. I was no longer afraid that the ghost of Mr. Tucker would show up. Now I was more afraid that he *wouldn't* show up. And what was Stuffy planning to do if he didn't? Once this night was over I might have a lot of explaining to do. If anyone was still talking to me.

But maybe they wouldn't find out. Maybe Stuffy could pull it off—whatever it was. Maybe everyone would have a really great, scary time, and never know the whole thing was a fake. Maybe it would turn out just as I'd hoped, with Sheila and Teddy and B. G. asking me to their parties, with Bonnie asking me to her house—

And maybe I'd grow wings and fly like a birdie.

At seven-twenty-five Stuffy came downstairs. "All set?" he asked.

"Are you?"

"You bet. Now look, I'll meet everybody at the door and direct them upstairs to the séance. You wait in the hall right outside the bedroom door. When we're all here we'll start the séance. And keep the bedroom door closed."

"Hold it. It's my party. At least, it was supposed to be. I should meet them at the door."

"But Wallis, you don't know them all. How will you be able to tell the crashers from the real guests? It's Hallowe'en—there'll be loads of people coming to the door."

"Then we can both meet them. I don't see why I have to stand upstairs—and why outside the bedroom?"

"It's for atmosphere," Stuffy said. "I want everyone to go in at the same time and not have any chance to talk or look around beforehand. You just keep them entertained in the hall until everyone's here."

"What do you want me to do, tap dance? Why can't we just wait down here and eat some of this stuff?" I waved toward the dining room table.

"Because that'll ruin the mood," Stuffy said impatiently.

The doorbell rang. My stomach jumped.

"Now, go on!" Stuffy hissed. "Hey, wait, where are your parents?"

"In the den. They promised to stay out of the way."

"Good, good! Go on, get upstairs."

Without thinking any more about it, except for a short, silent prayer, I ran upstairs and waited.

I heard voices at the door and moments later, feet trudging up the stairs. I realized that the hall light was off, though it had been on before. I reached to turn it on, but then stopped, thinking that the darkness might be part of Stuffy's "atmosphere."

"Wallis?" a voice whispered.

"Right here," I whispered back. I didn't know who it was.

"Why are we whispering?" whispered another voice. That one I recognized. It was B. G.

"B. G., is that you? Oh, there you are." I could see them now as they reached the top of the stairs. Enough light seeped up from the living room for me to recognize Sheila and Teddy as well as B. G.

"Why are you keeping it dark up here?" asked Sheila.

"I don't know. Stuffy said something about 'atmosphere.' Stuffy's running this whole thing, you know," I added. I hoped they'd remember I had said that when they discovered the séance was a fraud.

"It figures," muttered B. G. Teddy jabbed her with an elbow. What was that all about? I had no time to think about it, though, because the bell rang again and there were more footsteps heading our way.

"Arthur!" B. G. exclaimed. "What are you doing here?"

Arthur Deegan looked from one to the other of us without answering. Finally he said, "Same thing you are." He leaned against the wall and started whistling softly, as if he wasn't going to talk to us again.

"Oh, your coats," I said, noticing for the first time that they were all still bundled up. "Let me put them in the guest room." I took the girls' coats and looked toward Arthur. "Arthur, you want to give me your coat? I'll put it in the guest room."

He shook his head. "I'll keep it on."

In a few minutes the hall was packed with people; I really didn't have to entertain anyone because they were all chattering among themselves; the girls in excited whispers, the boys talking louder than usual as if to prove there was nothing to whisper about.

My stomach felt nervous and fluttery. I wished Stuffy would start already because the sooner we started, the sooner it would be over and I would know whether I had fifteen new friends or fifteen lifelong enemies.

I was so tense that it was a struggle to welcome Bonnie and Lynn, the last two people to arrive.

"I didn't know what to wear, Wallis," Lynn said as she handed me her coat. "What do you wear to a séance?"

"A sheet?" Ding Dong said. He laughed at that. No one else did.

"Why do we have to stand out here?" Bonnie asked.

"Stuffy wanted us all to go in together," I said.

"How come?"

"I don't know," I said. "Stuffy's running this whole thing. I don't know the first thing about having a séance. I just happen to have the house with the—possible—ghost."

"I feel like a sardine," Lynn said. "You know, it's crowded in here."

"No kidding?" said Packy. "You really mean it? I didn't notice." He was backed against a closet door, flattened out like he was trying to keep from being trampled to death by a surging mob.

It wasn't *that* bad.

Where was Stuffy?

"The séance is about to begin!" a voice announced.

"Finally," said B. G. So far, they weren't exactly having a ball at my party.

Everyone started talking at once, peppering Stuffy with questions.

"Quiet, *please!* We're going into the murder room now and we have to show a proper respect for the spirit we hope to call up. We don't want him to think we're just fooling around."

"Goodness, no," said Packy. "We might hurt his feelings."

Lynn giggled nervously.

"This is serious," Stuffy said sternly. He opened the door to my parents' bedroom and everyone pushed their way inside.

"It's cold in here!" Sheila said.

"Yeah, it is," agreed Eddie. "I'm freezing."

"I'm not," said Arthur Deegan.

"You're wearing your coat, Arthur," B. G. pointed out. "It *is* cold. Wallis, why is it so cold?"

Before I could answer, Teddy said, "All haunted houses have cold spots. I read that. There's always one spot in the house that you can't heat, no matter what you do. That's how you can tell that a spirit is present. Right, Stuffy?"

"Absolutely," said Stuffy. He sounded pleased. Why not? Teddy was doing half of his hype for him. I stepped into the room last. Stuffy had set up candles on the dresser, in those two silver candlesticks he had brought with him. They were the only light in the room. They flickered eerily in the mirror, like small, fiery diamonds, and cast shadows all over the wall behind the bed.

It *was* cold in there. Unearthly cold. Strange, but I'd never noticed a cold spot in my parents' room, and they'd certainly never said anything about it. Must have been part of Stuffy's preparations. But how? I looked over at the windows; the blinds were down.

I heard a faint, metallic ping. The sound was somehow familiar, but I couldn't remember why.

"Everyone sit down around the bed," Stuffy said. Obediently, we all squatted down in a semicircle, the girls clustering on one side of the bed and the boys on the other. Stuffy took his position on the boys' side, near the head of the bed, right in front of one of the night tables.

"We are about to begin," he announced. "Everyone clasp hands to make the magic circle."

Packy snorted. Eddie was the last boy in the circle before the line of girls and he had to hold hands with Sheila.

"I want to sit someplace else," he said. He started to get up.

"Oh, sit down, Ding Dong," Sheila snapped. "Don't be such a baby." She snatched his hand and pulled him down.

He grumbled something, but didn't argue. I sat between Lynn and a girl I recognized from class. Her name was Judy and she'd come with a friend whose name I couldn't remember. Nervously I took Judy's hand and joined hands with Lynn.

"This is so spooky," Lynn whispered eagerly.

"Quiet, please," said Stuffy. "We will begin. I want you all to close your eyes and call the spirit with me. Concentrate as hard as you can on contacting the spirit. Focus all your psychic energy on making a connection with the spirit of Mr. Tucker. Now say it with me: *Come to us, O troubled spirit.*"

"Come to us, O troubled spirit. Come to us, O troubled spirit." We repeated it over and over again, for what seemed like a long time. It began to sound eerie, all of us chanting that, like witches or something.

Suddenly there was a howling sound, as if the wind was blowly fiercely right there in the room.

Lynn's hand tightened on mine in a bone-breaking grip. "What's that?" she shrieked.

The howling got louder. It sounded like a regular Arctic blizzard. My heart started to pound. Was this part of Stuffy's act? I didn't know.

"Stuffy," Teddy squeaked, "what's that noise?"

"Shh!" Stuffy hissed. "This might be it." He sounded very tense. Maybe it wasn't part of his plans. How was I to know what was real and what was fake? I shivered.

"If you are there, O troubled spirit," Stuffy said, "please speak to us. We want to help you."

"*I* don't," said Ding Dong.

"Quiet!"

"I'm scared," Judy whispered.

"There's nothing to be—," I started. Then, suddenly, a gust of wind seemed to blow through the bedroom and the candles went out.

At least three people actually screamed and there was a confused babble of voices for a minute, until, cutting through the chatter like a knife, came the sound of a deep, slow voice.

"I . . . AM . . . HERE. . . ."

"Ohh, Bonnie." Lynn's voice. "*Wallis?*"

It was so dark in the room that I could barely see the outlines of the furniture.

Judy's teeth chattered. I could hear them when she leaned over and whispered in my ear, "I'm s-s-still sc-scared."

"Me too," I said.

———

I began to shiver. I didn't know if Stuffy was doing this. I had no way of being sure. The voice certainly wasn't Stuffy's—and it sounded like it was coming from so far away. Maybe it *was* the ghost of Mr. Tucker.

"Quiet, everyone!" Stuffy ordered. "Spirit, identify yourself please. We want to help you."

The howling sounds died down a little, but they still blew—the voice seemed to be fighting to be heard over the winds.

"I . . . AM . . . THE . . . OWNER . . . OF . . . THIS . . . HOUSE. . . . I . . . LIVE . . . HERE. . . ."

"Not anymore," said Arthur Deegan. He didn't sound very scared. Stuffy didn't sound that nervous anymore, either. Well, why should he? If he was doing the whole thing, most of us were scared enough so that he didn't have to worry. And if he wasn't, it was working out just fine as far as he was concerned. But I found that I was clutching Judy's hand as hard as she was clutching mine. Whether it was real or fake, it was plenty scary enough for me. In fact, I wanted to jump up, turn on the lights, and get everybody downstairs for refreshments. I'd had enough of the séance already.

"We want to help you," said Stuffy.

"H O W . . . W I L L . . . Y O U . . . HELP . . . ME . . . ?"

"We want to put your soul at rest. The people in this house mean you no harm. Your wife isn't here anymore."

"WHERE . . . IS . . . SHE . . . ?"

"In jail," Stuffy said. "For—uh—doing what she did."

"IS . . . SHE . . . HERE . . . ?"

"He doesn't hear very well, does he?" commented Packy.

"Oh, shut up," Teddy said. "Don't make fun of a troubled soul."

"Hard to hear over that wind," Arthur Deegan remarked.

"You shut up too, Arthur," ordered B. G.

The howling wind stopped.

"*Please*," said Stuffy. "This is no way to behave at a séance."

"Sorry," said Packy. "My mother never taught me how to behave at a séance."

"Packy, you can leave if you're not going to shut up," Stuffy said. "You're going to louse up the whole atmosphere with that attitude."

"Well, *excuse me*," Packy said. But he shut up.

Everyone got very quiet. And waited.

Softly the winds began to sound again. Then, gradually, they grew louder.

"Why do you hang around this house?" Stuffy asked. "You don't own it anymore."

"S H E . . . I S . . . N O T . . . A . . . G O O D . . . W O M A N . . . . S H E . . . SHOULD . . . BE . . . PUNISHED. . . ."

"She's in jail," Stuffy said. "She's being punished. You don't have to wait around to punish her. You leave Wallis and her family in peace and go rest your tortured soul."

"I . . . WAS . . . MURDERED. . . . I . . . MUST . . . BE . . . AVENGED. . . ."

One of the girls squealed.

That voice sounded so weird. If Stuffy had rigged this up, he had done a great job. It was scary even to me, even though I knew that it was a *possible* fake. In fact, I was almost sure of it now, because Stuffy couldn't have kept so calm if a ghost that he didn't believe in suddenly blew out the candles and started talking to us.

So it really had to be a fake ghost. Definitely, I told myself.

"You *are* avenged," Stuffy said. "And your murderer is in jail; she isn't here. So there's no reason for you to hang around here anymore. Go and live in peace."

"How can he live in peace?" muttered Ding Dong. "He's *dead*."

"GOODBYE . . . THEN. . . ."

The blowing winds got softer and softer, then faded out entirely.

"The séance is over!" announced Stuffy loudly. "You can unclasp hands now."

Everyone started talking at once. I got up to turn on the light, but before I got to the switch, the candles were suddenly sputtering again.

Everyone jumped as Stuffy blew out the match and smiled at them.

"Well, there you have it. Why don't we get something to eat," he suggested. "I'm starved."

"Sure," Packy said, "you had a big night. A séance and an exorcism all at the same time."

"Let's get out of here," said Eddie. "I'm hungry too."

"Yeah, fear always makes you hungry," said Packy.

"I wasn't scared!"

"For a person who wasn't scared, your hand sure sweated a lot," Sheila retorted.

"My hands always sweat," Eddie said. "I have very sweaty hands."

"You ought to use Right Guard," B. G. giggled.

I opened the bedroom door and everyone filed out, still talking about Mr. Tucker's ghost.

It had been great, just as Stuffy had promised. It really was a terrific séance. Now we would all have the refreshments, just like a party, and everything would be fine. I felt wonderful. Everyone was talking at once and when we got downstairs, B. G., Bonnie, Lynn, and Judy surrounded me, all telling me how scared they had been.

"So was I," I said truthfully. "I didn't even know for sure we had a ghost."

"Well, you don't have one anymore," Sheila said. "If you ever did."

"What do you mean, if she ever did?" Teddy asked.

I stopped pouring soda into paper cups and my hand started to shake. Sheila's voice was cold and disbelieving.

"She means," said Arthur, "that she doesn't believe in ghosts."

"Don't you, Sheila?" asked B. G. "You were plenty ready to come to the séance. Why did you come if you didn't think there'd be a real ghost?"

"For the same reason everyone came," said Sheila. "I was curious."

I forced myself to pour the soda again, trying to keep calm, trying not to panic. Sheila was going to ruin everything. I thought I might be sick.

"Well, if it wasn't a ghost," said Arthur, "it's the best imitation of one I ever heard."

I stared at him. Everyone stared at him—Sheila, Teddy, B. G., Bonnie. He'd never said so many words at once in front of anyone, and what words! I was sure he'd be the last person to believe in the phony—if it was phony—ghost, but he was sticking up for me.

That was it! He was sticking up for *me*. He didn't

believe that the ghost had been real, I was sure of that. But he was pretending that he did.

I gave him a grateful smile, and he grabbed a handful of thin pretzel sticks and stuffed them into his mouth all at once. He shoved his hands into his pockets.

Stuffy came over to the table and helped himself to handfuls of everything in sight.

"That was terrific, Stuffy," Lynn said. "You ran a great séance."

"Thank you," said Stuffy through a mouthful of Fritos.

"Was it real?" asked Bonnie.

I looked over at her. She didn't look angry or unbelieving. She just looked openly curious.

"Of course it was real," Stuffy said sloppily. "It was a real séance. I read up on them. That's how I knew what to do."

"Yeah, well how much did you do?" asked Packy.

Of course they didn't believe in Mr. Tucker's ghost. How could I have ever thought they would? What I should have said, right then and there, was, "Happy Hallowe'en! Wasn't that a great Hallowe'en stunt?"

But I didn't. I didn't say anything. I couldn't. It had gone too far.

"I was only the medium," Stuffy said. He was lying in his teeth. "I only served as the connecting link between us and the Beyond."

"And you were wonderful," Lynn said.

"Yeah, you were," Teddy agreed. "What was that howling sound, though? Was that wind?"

"It sounded so cold," B. G. said. She shivered

dramatically. "I hope that poor spirit isn't cold—wherever he is."

"Better cold than burning up," Packy pointed out.

I looked around. They were grabbing up the food like hungry vultures. They were having a good time. They had enjoyed the séance. The ones who didn't believe it didn't believe it—but they didn't care. The ones who wanted to believe would keep on believing no matter what the others said.

Stuffy had been right all along. They only wanted a good séance. That had been the important thing. Whether it was real or not didn't matter very much. As long as they enjoyed themselves.

And they did.

I went over to Stuffy, who was drinking paper cups of soda one after the other.

I had practically a room full of friends now—or at least, half a room full—and I felt absolutely wonderful. All these people were in my house, talking to me, drinking my soda, eating my potato chips, and having a good time as my guests, and it was all because of Stuffy. I might have been mad at him before, but now I felt so grateful I wanted to thank him.

"It was a wonderful séance, Stuffy," I said. "Really great."

"Thank you," he replied. "I think I did manage it pretty well. I mean, considering it was my first séance."

"You were terrific. And so was the—uh—ghost."

"Yeah. I never contacted a spirit before, so I think we were kind of lucky."

"Oh, I'm sure luck had nothing to do with it," I grinned.

Stuffy tried to look modest.

Then I remembered that little ping I had heard. Now I realized why it had sounded familiar. I had heard it before—lots of times. But not recently. It was the air conditioner. That was the sound that the air conditioner always made after it was turned off and while it was cooling down. Well, at least I knew how he had made the room cold. He probably turned off the radiator too.

But how had he done the gust of wind that blew out the candles? And where did the voice of Mr. Tucker come from? I couldn't ask him now, but I was sure going to. And soon.

The doorbell rang and I went to answer it. Three little kids were standing on the step. One was dressed like a witch, one like a ballet dancer, and one like a gypsy.

"Trick or treat!" they said together.

I turned to get some candy and found Sheila right at my shoulder.

She smiled nastily. I knew she was still thinking about the séance. "Trick," she said. "Definitely a trick."

FIFTEEN

Come on, Stuffy," I said. "I figured out most of it, like the air conditioner, and how you could use a tape recorder. But how did you get the candles to go out?"

"Shh. Here comes Ding Dong."

"Well hurry up and tell me, then."

We were on our way to school the next morning and I felt like nothing could stop me now. I was on my way up, life was going to be beautiful, and from here on I would be Wallis the Wonderful, with more friends than I could count.

What a beautiful day! It was gloomy gray, with a cold, misty drizzle. The sky looked filthy and my hair was going limp; the papers in my looseleaf were melting together, but I couldn't remember a more gorgeous day in my whole life.

"Tell me how you did that," I insisted. "How did you make a wind go through the room and blow out the candles?"

"What makes you think I did?" he said, under his breath. "Hi, Ding Dong."

Eddie trotted up to us. For a moment I felt a flash of annoyance; I had to know how Stuffy had done that thing with the candles. But my mood was so sunny that I felt a warm glow toward the whole world—even Ding Dong. I would find out later.

"Hi, Eddie!" I said cheerily.

"It's raining," he said.

I nodded. "That's true."

"How'd you like the séance, Ding Dong?" Stuffy asked.

Fishing for compliments, eh Stuffy? I thought.

"It was okay."

"Okay?" Stuffy snorted. "You were scared stiff."

"I was not."

"You were too."

"Was not."

"Were too."

This went on for about a block until I said, "Children, children, don't bicker."

We reached the school and for the first time it didn't look ugly and threatening. I felt almost a sort of affection toward it, like I wanted to pat its little yellow bricks as I walked up the steps. Since I couldn't reach its little yellow bricks, I patted its green metal doors instead. Not a bad school after all, I thought fondly. Even its missing L seemed kind of charming and quaint—a sweet little touch of vandalism.

I nearly giggled. I thought I might do a lot of

giggling today. After years full of days without the least reason to giggle, I had a lot of giggling stored up and ready to spill out.

Sheila, Teddy, and B. G. were already in their seats when I got into class.

"Hello!" I said, almost bubbling. B. G. and Teddy grinned and said, "Hi, Wallis!" Sheila said, "Hi," and didn't smile. She was still suspicious. At least she hadn't infected the other two.

In fact, they came over to my desk as I sat down, and started to talk excitedly about the séance.

"That was so scary, Wallis," Teddy said. "Do you think it was even scarier because you had it on Hallowe'en?"

Bonnie and Lynn came in and Lynn headed straight for my desk without even putting her coat away.

"Oh, Wallis, I was never so scared in my life! What a good séance that was."

A moment later Bonnie wandered over to join us. "Listen, Wallis," she said, "if I forgot to tell you, I had a really interesting time at the séance."

"You told me," I said. I flashed her a big smile. "Last night, before you left. Remember?"

An *interesting* time. I thought that was a funny way to put it. And she *had* told me last night—and used the same word. *Interesting*. Why didn't she just say she had a good time? Or thanks for asking me to your party?

Oh well. Maybe that was just Bonnie's way.

I looked around at all the friendly faces that surrounded me, like a protective wall around a castle. They *were* a protective wall, I thought. They were going to protect me against loneliness and friendliness and misery. I felt kind and generous and warm all over. I had never felt this way before in my life. I didn't feel the least bit *prickly*.

"What's going on?" Ruth pushed her way between Bonnie and Lynn and peered down at me.

Nobody said anything. I hadn't thought of Ruth once since Friday night. Now I felt guilty and secretive. She called me her best friend and now she was going to find out that she hadn't been invited to my party.

"Nothing, Ruth," I said. "We were just talking."

"About what?"

The other girls drifted away, leaving me to explain to Ruth whatever I could think up to explain to her.

For a minute I was mad at her for breaking up the group that had been gathered around my desk. I had been surrounded by love—or at least, *like*—for the first time in any school in any state in the country, and she had to come barging in and knock down my wall of friends.

But my anger dissolved and I felt sorry for her. I knew that if I talked to her now nobody was going to hold that against me. And there would be other days for people to cluster around my desk, or come to my house, or ask me to a party.

Arthur Deegan, who had been waiting for the girls to leave so he could sit down, slid into his seat.

"Hi, Arthur," I said warmly. I would never forget how he stood up for me last night. Maybe he did like me after all. I was afraid I was blushing, so I turned quickly to Ruth.

"Just talking about Hallowe'en," I told her. "Did you go trick or treating?"

Ruth shook her head. "I just took my sister around."

She leaned toward me and lowered her voice. "Did you mail—you know?"

I nodded. "Sure. I promised, didn't I?"

Her eyes were red-rimmed. Suddenly I wondered if she had been crying all weekend.

"Are you okay?"

"Yes. It's just—endings are so sad." She sighed. It sounded like something she'd read in a book.

She took her seat.

"What endings?" asked Arthur.

"Oh—just endings in general, I guess."

I looked down at my desk, feeling so self-conscious that I couldn't look at Arthur.

There on the desk were two brand-new ball-point pens.

"What—"

I owed you. I borrowed pens from you."

"Yeah, but—"

"Well, I didn't always remember to give them back," Arthur said.

"But these are much better than the ones I lent you," I protested. "You really shouldn't have."

"That's okay."

I managed to smile directly at him. "Well, thank you, Arthur."

He turned away and busied himself with his books. " 'S okay."

"Wallis! Wallis! Over here!" Teddy waved at me and I carried my tray over to her table. I didn't see Bonnie and Lynn anywhere, but even if I had, I knew I would have gone to sit with Sheila, Teddy, and B. G.

Sheila nodded coolly as I sat down, but Teddy and

B. G. seemed really glad to have me eat with them. They were still talking about the séance. I had the suddenly uncomfortable feeling that Sheila was watching me carefully, as if she expected me to make a wrong move at any moment and was waiting to catch me in it.

"Well, you know, the séance part was Stuffy's idea. I really thought of it as more of a party, but Stuffy thought it would be exciting to have a séance too."

"A party?" Sheila repeated slowly, as if she weren't sure she'd heard right.

"Yeah. You know, for Hallowe'en."

"Do you always," Sheila asked, her voice dangerously calm, "sell tickets to your parties?"

I nearly choked on my tunafish.

"Sheila, you promised!" B. G. growled.

"I didn't promise anything," Sheila said. "You and Teddy promised, but I didn't."

I dropped my sandwich on my tray, suddenly feeling like I was going to keel over. The whole room got fuzzy. I looked at the three girls, but I couldn't get them in focus. Was I going to faint?

Sell tickets? What in the world were they talking about?

"I didn't sell tickets," I managed to whisper. "I don't know anything about any tickets."

"You see? I told you she didn't know about it," said Teddy. "It was another one of Stuffy's—*schemes.*"

"How do you know she didn't know?" Sheila demanded. "Just because she says so?"

"*Stuffy sold tickets?*" I could hardly say it.

"A dollar a ticket," Sheila said. "As if you didn't know."

"*I didn't!*" I couldn't believe this was happening.

How could he do it to me? I thought he was my *friend*.

Yet now, thinking about it, even through my shock and confusion, I *could* believe it. It explained so much. It explained *everything*.

Teddy and Sheila were still talking but I wasn't hearing them. I was recalling the whole week leading up to the séance, replaying it in my mind, finally understanding all the things that had seemed so strange.

Stuffy had made the invitations and sent them. The one he showed me was a *sample*. He must have added things to it before he mailed it.

And maybe he purposely mailed them so late that no one would have a chance to talk to me about the séance beforehand. And that's why he wanted so many people. Fifteen people at a dollar a head was fifteen dollars' profit for Stuffy.

And I thought he was doing it to help me make friends!

It was a miracle anyone was *talking* to me, let alone being friendly.

That was what Lynn meant about the séance being "worth it." And why shouldn't Sheila be cold and suspicious? If she paid for a séance, she had the right to expect a real séance, not just some phony con game.

And Stuffy telling me he had to answer the door to keep crashers from trying to get into my "party." He had to answer the door to take the money. That's why he didn't want me around to greet my "guests."

I jumped up from the table, leaving my lunch tray where it was.

"Wallis, where are you—"

I ignored Teddy. Blinking hard so I wouldn't cry, I bumped into someone.

"Wallis, can I sit here?"

It was Ruth.

"Yeah," I said, "but I have to go."

I pushed past her and shook my head, trying to clear my eyes. I had to find Stuffy. He had gotten me into this and he was going to have to get me out.

I didn't see him at any of the tables. I wiped my eyes on my sleeve and walked all around the lunchroom, checking every single table to make sure I didn't miss him.

I wasn't the slightest bit hungry. I was much too angry to think about food, and I probably would have been sick if I even looked at my tunafish sandwich.

I finally saw him coming off the lunch line, carrying a loaded tray.

I stormed over to him and grabbed his arm. I was nearly ready to burst into tears.

"Hey, watch it, Wallis. You almost made me drop the tray."

"Stuffy, how could you? How could you play such a rotten trick on me?"

That did it. Now I was crying. I wiped my eyes and bit my lip hard, trying to stop myself.

"Uh oh."

"Is that all you can say?" I choked. "You better say more than that."

"Aw, Wallis, it was just for fun."

"It was just for *money*. If it was just for fun, you wouldn't have sold tickets."

"But everybody had a good time. And look at all the friends you have now."

"Stuffy, if Sheila convinces everybody that I was in on this, I'm not going to have *any* friends. Now you're going to come with me and tell them the truth."

I practically dragged him over to the table where Ruth was eating, silently, opposite Sheila, Teddy, and B. G. "Watch my tray," he kept yelling. "Watch it, will you?"

"Tell them," I said. I took a deep breath and sniffled in, hard. "Tell them the truth."

The girls looked up at us and for a moment I was sorry that Ruth had to be around to hear about my séance this way. But she would have found out sooner or later, and before Sheila had a chance to turn everyone against me, I wanted Stuffy to come clean.

"Wallis didn't have anything to do with charging money," Stuffy said. "That was my idea."

"You see?" B. G. said to Sheila. "Now do you believe it?"

"Why should I?" Sheila asked. "Maybe that was part of their agreement."

"But why didn't you ask me?" I said. "Why didn't you call me up or something, and ask about the tickets?"

Ruth was looking from face to face, bewildered. "What tickets?" No one answered her. She lowered her pale eyes and examined her sandwich.

"Because Stuffy told us not to," Teddy said.

"He said talking about money with the person nearest the spirit would put a bad aura on the séance and the spirit might not want to show up," B. G. explained.

"Is *that* what you told them?" I asked Stuffy.

He nodded.

How could they have believed such a phony story? I'm sure I wouldn't have.

"Sheila," Teddy said suddenly, "if Wallis was in on it, why did Stuffy make so sure we wouldn't talk about the séance with her?"

"Hey, yeah, Sheila," B. G. chimed in. "If Wallis knew Stuffy was selling tickets all along, he wouldn't have had to say that about money talk lousing up the aura."

I turned to Sheila. She was quiet, thoughtful. She looked like a judge about to hand down a decision in a murder case. I felt like the criminal being tried. Everything seemed to depend on what the judge—Sheila—decided.

"Wallis really didn't know anything about the money," Stuffy said. "And I purposely sent the invitations late so you wouldn't have too much chance to talk to her before."

So I was right about *that* part.

"And the reason I didn't want you to talk to her about it," Stuffy went on, "was because I knew if she knew, she'd never let me do it."

"Of course she wouldn't have," Teddy said.

"And Stuffy's going to give you all back your money," I said firmly. "Aren't you, Stuffy?"

"What?" he howled.

"You're going to give back their money," I hissed.

"Why should I?" argued Stuffy. "They got what they paid for."

"It's okay, Wallis," Sheila said suddenly. "He's right. We knew what we were doing."

I stared at Sheila. The judge had made her decision;

the court was going to be merciful. I couldn't believe my ears.

"We should be used to Stuffy's—uh—*projects* by now. But you couldn't have known. You're new." She turned to B. G. "Remember 'Consolidated Snuggle Bug'?"

"Ohh, how could I forget?" B. G. groaned.

Stuffy beamed happily, as if he were recalling one of his great triumphs.

"That was Stuffy's slipper-sock company," Sheila went on. "Last year we did a unit on the stock market and how to invest in a company, and Stuffy told us he was forming a corporation to make slipper socks."

"It was one of my best things," Stuffy sighed.

Sheila glared at him. "Anyway, he told us there were these little old ladies in Duluth, Minnesota, who were knitting the slipper socks for twenty-five cents a pair, and he would sell them at five dollars a pair, so we'd make a fortune in slipper socks. But he needed stockholders to buy shares and with the money from the shares, he could pay for the wool that the little old ladies would knit the slipper socks with."

"And you bought shares?" I asked.

"I bought ten shares at fifty cents a share," B. G. moaned.

"So did I," Ruth said softly.

"What happened?"

"Well, we all bought shares—and kept buying them. But when it came time for our first dividend, Stuffy told us that we had to reinvest the money in the company because the only way we'd make a killing in slipper socks was by selling thousands of pairs. Anyway, we finally found out there were no little old ladies in Duluth, and the whole company was a fake.

The only thing 'Consolidated Snuggle Bug' ever made were the stock certificates Stuffy gave us."

"But they were beautiful," Teddy pointed out. "I still have mine."

"It would have worked," Stuffy protested. "I just had trouble finding the right little old ladies. If you'd left your money in the company just a little bit longer—"

"Oh, come on, Stuffy! We never got our money *out* of the company!"

"I had expenses," Stuffy said.

"Yeah," said Sheila. "Getting those certificates made up. Anyway, that's just one of Stuffy's great ideas; so we really should have known what we were getting into, Wallis, when we paid Stuffy to come to your séance."

I stared at Stuffy. "Just one of your ideas? You mean, there are more?"

"Sure," said Stuffy. "I'll tell you all about them. There was the time I—"

"Never mind," I snapped. I thought of the worm wrestling and the letters to Ruth. And I reminded myself that even though everything was going to be all right now, I was still mad at him. I'd had enough of Stuffy's "ideas" for awhile.

"Lunch hour's practically over and we have about ten more people for you to apologize to. Let's go." Stuffy sighed heavily and picked up his tray.

"See you later, Wallis," Sheila said. I wanted to leap up and cheer, hearing that. I was finally, definitely, going to be accepted.

Ruth looked up at me. Her face was sad and resigned. I knew she must be thinking that if I was friends with Sheila, Teddy, and B. G., I'd never speak to her, except to make fun of her like they did. I hesitated a moment, then said, "See you later, Sheila. You too, Ruth."

Ruth's mouth opened in a wide, surprised smile. It was full of Oreo crumbs.

S I X T E E N

T hat was a great movie," Lynn sighed.

"I thought it was silly," Bonnie said.

"Oh, come on," Lynn giggled. "You were as scared as I was."

"I wasn't a bit scared," Bonnie protested. "Not one bit."

"Then why'd you spill your popcorn all over your lap?"

"Wallis jiggled my hand."

"I did not," I laughed. "And you were as scared as we were."

We stopped in front of the poster showing a scene from the movie. The star was a girl about our age, and the poster showed a ghastly, corpselike hag rising above the girl's shoulders, as if it were coming out of her body.

"I don't know why they called it 'Demon in My Pocket,' though," Lynn said. "It was never in her pocket."

"You want to stop for pizza?" asked Bonnie.

"Why don't you come to my house and we'll have cocoa or something?" I suggested comfortably. "It's close."

"Oh, good," said Lynn. "Let's go to Wallis's."

We linked arms and started the cold walk home from the shopping center.

It was three months since the séance, and I felt like I was living in a dream. I'd been to a pajama party at B. G.'s, a birthday party at Sheila's, and had gone skating twice with Sheila, B. G., and Teddy. I'd been to Bonnie's house and Lynn's, more times than I could count. It was too good to be true, which was why I always felt like I must be dreaming. If this is a dream, I kept telling myself, I want to spend the rest of my life asleep.

My mother and father were on the phone almost every evening talking to Grandma. Even though I knew they were telling her all about the friends I was seeing, I would get on the phone afterwards and tell her again myself. She always sounded so happy.

Lynn was still talking about the movie when we got to my house. We made cocoa and took it up to my room.

"That's just the kind of part I want to play when I'm an actress," Lynn said.

"You say that after every movie you see," Bonnie teased.

"I'd rather play really tragic parts," I said. "Like the girl whose lover is killed in the war, or where I have this fatal illness and I die bravely and beautifully and all my loved ones are inspired by my courage."

Lynn's eyes shone. "Oh, that sounds neat. I'd like to play a part like that too."

"See?" Bonnie laughed. "I told you."

"Oh, shut up," said Lynn. "But you have to suffer to play tragic parts. I haven't suffered enough yet. Maybe I will some day, though," she said hopefully.

"I have," I muttered.

"Oh, Wallis, you have not. You're just a kid. You haven't *really* suffered."

Want to bet?

Of course, it was hard to think about suffering now, when I was so happy. But I *had* suffered. And I knew that even a kid could suffer. And you didn't have to be beaten or abandoned in a snowstorm or sent to work in the coal mines to suffer either.

Bonnie and Lynn left just before dinner. Moments after they went home, my father came in, with Grandma right behind him.

"Grandma, I didn't know you were coming!" I threw my arms around her. I couldn't get them all the way around, because she was wearing this enormous plaid coat, with a cape or something attached, so there was even more of Grandma than usual.

"Surprise, surprise," she said. I looked up at her face. She was smiling, but her smile seemed strained, just as her cheerfulness had sounded sort of forced.

My mother came in from the kitchen. "Well, well, Mother," she said, her voice bright. "You're just in time for dinner."

Something was wrong.

I looked from one face to the other and for an eerie

moment they all seemed to be wearing masks. Like the masks of comedy and tragedy that stand for the theater—they were all wearing the mask of comedy, with broad, fixed smiles and blank, empty eyeholes.

"What is it?" I cried. "Why are you acting like this? Why is Grandma here?"

"Why shouldn't I be here?" Grandma asked. "Don't you want me to visit?"

"Yes, but you didn't just come to visit," I said wildly. "Something's going on—I know it. You're all hiding something!"

Then, suddenly, without anyone saying a word, I knew what was happening. My three-month dream was over. It was time to wake up.

"I knew it," I wailed. "I knew it was too good to last. That's it, isn't it? We have to move again."

"Wallis, I—" my father began.

"Honey—" my mother said.

"Don't honey me!" I shouted. "Am I right? Just tell me if I'm right?"

"Well, yes, but—"

"How could you?" I shrieked. "How could you do this to me now, *again*?" My eyes were blind with tears, and I pushed past my mother and dashed upstairs, stumbling near the top so I had to grab for the banister to keep from falling.

I ran into my room and slammed the door. I threw myself onto the bed, knocking over a mostly empty cup of cocoa on my night table. I heard the cup roll across the table and stop. I knew the remains of the cocoa must be sloshing over the side of the floor, probably ruining the table and my blue rug beneath. Good. I hoped they *would* be ruined.

———

I was crying so hard the bed shook with my sobs. For the first time in my life I had friends. I was happy. Couldn't they stand to see me happy? Was three months of happiness all I was going to be allowed in my *whole life?*

There was a knock on the door. I ignored it. But the door opened anyway.

"Wallis?"

It was Grandma.

"Wallis, honey, I know how you feel."

"No you don't! You're on their side. You're part of it. You knew all along, before anybody told *me.*"

I shouted all this into my pillow. I don't know how much of it she could understand, because it came out muffled, but I wouldn't look at her.

"Well, whether you want to hear it or not, I'm going to try and explain things to you so you'll understand the situation. No one *wants* you to be unhappy. Your mother and father are as upset about this as you are."

Oh, sure. But we're moving anyway.

"A vice-president in the West Coast office had a heart attack and he was told he had to stop working for a while, so he took early retirement. Your father is going to replace him. As a *vice-president* of the company, Wallis. You know what that means?"

Sure. Lots of money. Big deal.

"That means that he's finally got the job he's been working toward all these years. But much sooner than he expected. It's practically unheard-of for a man his age to be a vice-president."

Goody for him. What did I care about his success? Every promotion he got meant more unhappiness for me. It was the story of my life.

"It means," Grandma went on, "that you won't have to move again. That is it. The last move. He's gotten what he's been aiming at."

"But I don't want to move!" I sobbed. "I want to stay here."

"You're happy here, aren't you, Wallis?"

"Yes!" I wailed. I buried my head in the pillow. With my eyes shut tight I could see the faces of all the friends I'd made passing in front of me one by one. It was such a *long* line—I would never have so many friends again. This was a fluke, an accident. There'd never be another Stuffy Sternwood to give a séance for me. It would be like all the other times, in Denver, in San Francisco, in Philadelphia, in Indianapolis. Only this time it would be permanent—and my misery would be forever.

"But you weren't happy here at first, were you?"

I didn't answer. I knew what she was getting at. I'd get used to the next place and make friends, just like I had here, she was going to say. But I wouldn't.

"Maybe it's selfish of me," she went on, "but I'm so happy about this move. I've always wanted to live in California, ever since I was out there in nineteen forty-nine. And now that you'll be settled, I'm finally going to do it."

"You're moving?" I said at last, turning over to look at her. "With us?"

"Well, I won't live with you, of course, but I'll find a place nearby. It's like a dream come true for me." She sighed. I suspected she was thinking of the Farmers' Market and wishing Clark Gable was still alive.

"And you'll be right near Grandma and Grandpa Todd," she said. "Think how nice that'll be for them.

And for your mother, to be close to her parents again. The whole family will be together."

Think how nice it will be for everyone—except me. Nobody seemed to care how it would be for Wallis. Nobody worried about what I wanted. California— 3,000 miles from Briar Ane School. At last my father could root for the Dodgers again. Terrific.

"Honey, you made friends here. You thought you couldn't, but you did. And if you made friends here, you can make friends anywhere. It's not something that only happens in one place."

"Oh, yes, it is. This is the only place it ever happened in."

"This is the *first* place it happened in," Grandma corrected me. "That's the thing. You've learned how to make friends now. You must have. Because you wouldn't have so many friends if you hadn't."

"It's only because of Stuffy and the séance and this house," I insisted. "We'll never get another house with a murdered ghost in it."

She laughed. "Wallis, you were hysterical when you found out about the murder! Don't you remember?"

"Well, it turned out better than I expected."

"Maybe your parents can find another house where someone was murdered," she smiled. "In California."

I shook my head. "I'd never get that lucky twice."

She put her hand over her mouth. I could tell she was trying not to laugh. I didn't think it was funny; it was the truth.

"After the séance," she pointed out, "those people must have decided they liked you, or else they wouldn't have kept calling you and inviting you to their houses, right?"

I shrugged.

"Well? Am I right?"

I didn't answer. I was thinking. It was true that Sheila and Teddy and B. G. hadn't been very friendly before the séance, but Bonnie and Lynn had. And Stuffy had been friends with me from the first day I met him. And Ruth—well, forget Ruth.

And after the séance, even when they had been conned out of a dollar for it, Teddy and B. G. at least were still willing to be friends with me. Even Sheila, eventually. And they didn't *have* to be. I mean, why should they ask me to their parties, and to go skating with them, if they didn't like me? Just because I had invited them to one séance at my house—for which they had to *pay admission*—didn't mean they had to ask me to all those other things afterwards.

They *liked* me.

And if they liked me, that meant other people might like me.

But to start all over again! And so soon. To have to face *another* new school, a new sea of strange faces, the explanations about my name. It was too much. Too much of them to ask, to much of them to expect of me.

The tears, which had stopped, started again.

"You could always give another séance," Grandma suggested. "Not that I think you should," she added hastily. "But maybe a party—you could give a party and—"

I was crying so hard I didn't hear the rest. I didn't go down for dinner either. I just might, I thought bitterly, never eat again. If the choice was between starving to death and moving to California, I would just as soon starve. At least I would have friends around me when I breathed my last breath.

SEVENTEEN

Oh, Wallis, that's awful!"

Lynn looked absolutely miserable. "Isn't that awful, Bonnie?"

Bonnie just nodded. It was like she didn't know what to say.

"But you just got here," Lynn said. "It's not *fair*."

"I know," I muttered. Bonnie patted my hand. "I know how you feel," she said. She did, too. It wasn't like Grandma or my mother saying it. Bonnie had *been* there. After all, she was new here just last year.

I was finally telling people. I hadn't said anything at first because I didn't want to spoil everything, but now it looked like we'd be moving in March and I had to tell them. Maybe I'd been hoping that if I didn't believe it, wouldn't accept it, it would never happen. But it was happening.

"I'll never have such good friends again," I said.

"Oh, Wallis!" Lynn wailed.

"Yes you will," Bonnie said. "You'll see. It'll work out."

I shook my head.

Earlier that morning I had told Sheila, Teddy, and B. G. Teddy had looked sad. B. G. looked positively annoyed at my parents for doing this to me. Sheila had just clucked sympathetically and said, "That's rough." Sheila wouldn't lose any sleep over my leaving, but I knew the others were sorry to see me go, and that was a little comforting. I had been about to leave Sheila's house to go on to Ruth's when B. G. stopped me at the door. She looked around carefully, as if to make sure no one was listening, then whispered, "My middle name is Grace. Don't tell anyone."

I smiled weakly. "Who am I going to tell?" I asked. "I won't be here."

"Bianca Grace," B. G. mused, as if I hadn't spoken. "Isn't that the most awful thing you ever heard?"

"The second most awful thing," I replied.

I had to go see Ruth next. I still had guilt pangs about not having invited her to the séance, and I even felt guilty because I'd never tried to like her—even though she didn't know how much I *dis*liked her. But now that I was moving and didn't have to worry about her pressuring me all the time to be friends, I could at least be a *little* nice to her before I left.

She was miserable over the news. When I told her, her face seemed to crumple and I thought she was going to cry.

"Oh, no," she whimpered. "Oh, Wallis, I don't believe it! It's not *fair*."

"I know it. I don't think so either."

She turned away from me and sat hunched over on her rug. Her sweater hitched up from her slacks and I could see several inches of pasty white skin above her waistband.

"You, you'll always make friends," she whispered. "But me—you're practically the only friend I ever had. It's not *fair*."

"Aw, Ruth. . . ." How could she say that? I was no friend at all. The last time she had called me her best friend I had been embarrassed because she didn't know what a rotten trick I'd played on her with those letters of Stuffy's. And now she was doing it again, when I was only here because I felt guilty, not because I liked her.

And how could she think I'd always make friends? That was the stupidest thing I ever heard. It figured Ruth would think that. It just went to show how little she really knew about what I was like.

"I'll write to you, Wallis," she promised as I left. "You write first, though, and tell me your address."

I nodded.

"I'll really miss you," she said.

"Well, I'm not leaving yet, Ruth," I said irritably. "Not for a month." But she meant it. And I was sure that she'd keep her word about writing to me, even if not one other person from Briar Ane School ever did.

And now I'd told Bonnie and Lynn and the only person left to tell was Stuffy.

"It'll work out," Bonnie said again. "You think it won't now, but you'll see. You can make new friends, Wallis. I mean, just look at how Sheila and her group accepted you. And they don't let hardly *anybody* into their exclusive little clique."

For just a moment I thought Bonnie was jealous. Her

voice sounded sarcastic when she said that about Sheila. But I guess I imagined it.

"Do you really think so?" It didn't matter what my mother or my father or Grandma said. They didn't know. But Bonnie was my own age. She knew. She knew what I was like and how other kids felt about me and she knew how hard it was to go to a new school. She could tell me the truth.

"You really think I'll be able to make friends?"

"Oh, Wallis, I'm sure of it. We'll miss you a lot more than you'll miss us."

I wanted to believe her. Maybe Ruth wasn't smart, but Bonnie was. It had sounded stupid when Ruth said it, about my being able to make friends, but now Bonnie was saying it too. Could they be right?

Bonnie's mother drove me home. As I got out of the car, I saw Stuffy sitting on my front steps, next to a small pile of graying snow.

"You'll get wet," I warned. "It's all melting."

I hadn't seen him much at all since I made him pay everyone back after the séance. I'd been too busy with all the new friends he'd helped me make. I had told him about writing the letter for Ruth, and I insisted that the "joke" was over. He was bored with the letters, anyhow, and was developing a brand new idea. It was a contest, with entry fees. He was planning a huge spelling bee, with a dollar charge to participate, and the grand prize would come out of the entry fees. Of course, if no one was able to spell the last word, no one would win the grand prize. . . .

"Look at this," he said. He held out a small red woolen glove. "Look inside." I looked inside and nearly jumped out of my skin. There were worms in two of the fingers.

"Oh, Stuffy!" I shoved the glove back at him. "Ricardo and Lola?" I asked, still shaken by the wormy glove.

"Funk and Wagnalls," he corrected. "They're going to be acrobats. I think they're naturals on a tightrope."

"Why the glove?"

"It's cold out! Haven't you noticed?"

"Oh, yeah," I said. "Want to come in?"

"Are you really moving?"

"How did you know?" I asked. "I hardly told anyone."

"Bad news travels fast around here," he said glumly. "You *are* moving?"

"Yeah. I was just going to tell you. But how did you find out?"

"Arthur Deegan asked me if it was true. That was the first I heard about it."

"But how did Arthur Deegan know?"

"He said he saw Teddy at the shopping center and she told him."

"Oh."

"California, huh?"

"Yeah. Near Los Angeles."

"That stinks," he muttered.

"You said it. You know, even if I was mad at you about the séance, you were right about all the friends I made from it. I never could have done that without you."

"Oh, that," he said. He waved his hand carelessly. "You would have made friends anyhow. They liked you before the séance."

"They *did?*"

"Sure."

"Then why did you tell me—"

"Because I wanted you to have the séance," he said impatiently. "And I knew if I told you you'd make a lot of friends that way, you'd do it. That was what you call my ace in the hole. But they would have been your friends anyway. Eventually."

"Ohh, Stuffy!"

I tried very hard to be angry at him.

But I couldn't. First Ruth, then Bonnie, now Stuffy was saying that I could make friends on my own now, that I didn't need a séance or a haunted house or a gimmick or *anything*. Even if you didn't count Ruth . . .

"Yeah, I'll be sorry to see you go," Stuffy was saying. "You have real imagination—and vision, like me. Those letters we sent to Ruth—hey, how about one more, for old times' sake?"

"No," I said firmly. "I told you no more, and you agreed."

"Oh well." He sighed.

I suddenly realized that there were an awful lot of people who were sorry to see me go.

I wonder if my friends in California will be this nice? I thought. And then, startled, I looked up at Stuffy. He was curling either Funk or Wagnalls around his finger, but that wasn't what startled me.

"What's the matter?" he asked.

"Nothing. I was just thinking."

I had thought, "my friends in California" automatically—before I even realized I was thinking it. Like I *knew* I would have friends in California. For the first time, the very first time ever, I expected to have friends in my new school. And the minute I realized that, I knew it was going to happen. Because I would make it happen. I *could* make it happen. Everyone thought so; and, most of all, now *I* thought so too.

I started up the steps. Then I remembered what I'd been trying to find out for months. "Stuffy, you never told me how you blew those candles out."

He hesitated a moment. Then he spoke, so softly I could hardly hear him. "I didn't."

"You *didn't?* They blew out . . . by themselves?"

"I guess. Unless . . . someone else blew them out."

I stood at the front door, trying to understand. I had my hand on the doorknob when Stuffy called after me in his normal voice, "By the way. Arthur Deegan likes you."

I shook myself. The eerie moment had passed. I smiled happily.

"I know it," I said, and went into the house.

ABOUT
THE AUTHOR

ELLEN CONFORD has written many books for young adults, including *Hail, Hail Camp Timberwood* and *The Things I Did for Love*. Mrs. Conford is a championship-level Scrabble player and competes in crossword puzzle tournaments. She and her husband live in Great Neck, New York.